Praise for

MONSTERS IN APPALACHIA

"*Monsters in Appalachia* is wildly outrageous at times, but there is empathy in these stories as well. Humor and sadness achieve a delicate balance."

—Ron Rash, author of *The Cove* and *Above the Waterfall*

"A memorable debut: each of these stories is as original and multidimensional as the characters who inhabit them."

—*Kirkus* (starred review)

"Monks knows her monsters, both literal and figurative. And she knows the territory of hills and hollers, where reality is sometimes heightened so sharply that it bleeds into myth. . . . These stories sparkle with dark, extreme humor."

—*Publishers Weekly* (starred review)

"A fresh, new voice in contemporary fiction, in stories of teenage angst, bonds of family, motherhood, and contradictions of middle age. Always surprising, these stories conjure both sorrow and mystery with intimate, loving detail."

—Robert Morgan, author of *Gap Creek*, *Chasing the North Star*, and *Boone: A Biography*

"These elemental stories take on the dark Appalachian territory of David Joy and Ron Rash with a kind of raw, absolute, female confidence. Coal miners, snake handlers, smart, scary women at their wits' end—all at the mercy of their terrific landscape. *Monsters in Appalachia* offers a glimpse of the edge of a world that seems freshly electric, and treacherous as hell."

—Ashley Warlick, author of *The Arrangement*

"Sheryl Monks's stories are gorgeously written dispatches from Appalachia, telling the difficult truth of what it is to survive in a place that can exact a heavy price. But these tales are generous too, and a particular grace sets on them all."

—Charles Dodd White, author of *A Shelter of Others*
and *Sinners of Sanction County*

"Haunting, raw, terrifying, and passionate."

—Sara Pritchard, author of
Help Wanted: Female and *Crackpots*

"There's music in these stories—visceral, rhythmical, soulful, deep. They are siren songs, taking us places we otherwise might not go."

—Kim Church, author of *Byrd*

"Sheryl Monks writes with unflinching honesty and deep affection about the Appalachia I know: a place of imminent peril to both body and soul, home to lingering ghosts. Her gorgeous (but never merely decorative) language generously limns the hard mountain landscape as well as the luminously realized and all-too-human folks who struggle there. This collection brought me home again."

—Pinckney Benedict, author of *Miracle Boy*
and Other Stories

"Sheryl Monks gives us such a range and depth of character in one collection. Her stories continue to delight and haunt long after reading."

—Renée K. Nicholson, author of *Roundabout Directions*
to Lincoln Center

MONSTERS IN
APPALACHIA

—

STORIES

—

Sheryl Monks

VANDALIA PRESS

MORGANTOWN 2016

First edition published 2016 by Vandalia Press, an imprint of West Virginia
University Press
Printed in the United States of America

ISBN:
paper 978-1-943665-39-6
epub 978-1-943665-40-2
pdf 978-1-943665-41-9

Library of Congress Cataloging-in-Publication Data is available from the
Library of Congress

Book and cover design by Than Saffel

Stories in this collection previously appeared in the following journals:
"Burning Slag" appeared in *The Butter*, May 2015.
"Robbing Pillars" appeared in *Split Lip Magazine*, July 2016.
"The Immortal Jesse James" appeared in *Midwestern Gothic*, Issue 5, Spring
2012.
"Barry Gibb Is the Cutest Bee Gee" appeared, in a slightly different form, in
Greensboro Review, Number 92, Fall 2012, and was nominated by editor Jim
Clark for the anthology series *New Stories from the South*.
"A Girl at His Show" appeared in *Backwards City Review*, Vol. 2, No. 2/Issue 4,
Fall 2006, and was a finalist in the 2006 *Backwards City Review* fiction contest.
In October 2009, the story was anthologized in *Surreal South '09*.
"Run, Little Girl" was a finalist in the 2006 fiction contest sponsored by
VERB: An Audio Quarterly, and first appeared in *Night Train*, Issue 10.1, May
2010. It was republished in *Black and Grey magazine*, July 10, 2012, and
anthologized in *Night Train: The First Ten Years*.
"Little Miss Bobcat" won the 2003 Reynolds Price Short Fiction Award
judged by Shannon Ravenel, and appeared in *RE:AL—Regarding Arts & Letters*,
Vol. 30.2, Fall/Winter 2006.
"Justice Boys" appeared, in a slightly different form, in *Fried Chicken and
Coffee: A Blogazine of Rural and Appalachian Literature* in July 2009, and was
named a Notable Story of 2009 by the *storySouth* Million Writers Award
competition in April 2010.
"Monsters in Appalachia" appeared in *storySouth*, Issue 30, Fall 2010, and was
later anthologized in *Surreal South '11: Monsters and Ghosts*.
Some stories in this collection also appeared in *All the Girls in France*, which
was named a finalist for the Hudson Prize, sponsored by Black Lawrence
Press, in November 2013.

For Mom and Dad.
And for Bruce.

Contents

Acknowledgments

——

I'm grateful to the storytellers in my family who instilled in me the love of narrative: my parents, my paternal grandmother, uncles, aunts, cousins. I'm especially indebted to my mom, who continues to inspire and encourage me, who faithfully holds onto the family stories and fuels my imagination with their retelling. To my sister and brother, who have always indulged me when I ask them to let me run a new story by them. To my brother-in-law, Danny, who helped me with details about the particulars of mill work. To nephews and nieces, Jordan Brown, Savannah Stanley, Luke Brown, Carter Mabry, and Emma Mabry, for simply being themselves and making my life happier. To Bruce, who supported me in every way a person can be supported. To my father, who is the reason I started writing at all. To Lincoln, who never left my side.

I'm deeply appreciative of friends and fellow writers who have over the years offered critical feedback that helped me craft many of the stories in this book. I've been fortunate to have belonged to two supportive and faithful writing groups and to have formed strong bonds with many other fellow writers who have contributed in so many ways to my writing life. Priscilla Bourgoine, Gwynyth Mislin, Rosemary Jones, Susan Woodring, Karen McBryde, WOWettes, sisters: you know all my stories. Jane McBryde, without whom WOW may never have been sustained. Ginger Hendricks, Joy Beshears, and Penny Niven: beyond words. I can't even express all you mean to me. Jennifer Niven and Lynda Black with whom I've exchanged work and formed deep friendships over the years. *Change Seven* friends who have given so selflessly to me and other writers: Antonios Maltezos, Laurel Dowswell, Emily Ramser, Chelsei Crotteau, Priscilla Bourgoine, Eric Rampson, Shannon Henesy, Corey Mesler, Laura Jean Moore, Joseph Mills, Susan Woodring, Kelly Davio, Tom Darin Liskey, Anne Weisgerber, Kristina Moriconi, Sandy Ebner, Jody Hobbs Hesler, Charlie Nickles, Andrea Fekete, Pat Berryhill, L. N. Holmes. To mentors, teachers, and editors who have supported my work: Penelope Niven, John Ehle, Ann Pancake, Pinckney Benedict, Ashley Warlick, David Payne, Elissa Schappell, Jenny Offill, Fred Leebron, Ron Rash, Edyta Oczkowicz, Janet Zehr, Jo Dulan, Annette Allen, Jim Clark, Terry Kennedy, Rusty Barnes, Sheldon Lee Compton, Roxane Gay. To friends in the North Carolina writing community who have offered support: Ed Southern and everyone at the NC Writers' Network; Cathy McKenzie, Susan Lyons, and so many others in the North Carolina Arts Council community; Ginger Hendricks, Jamie Southern, and everyone at Bookmarks; Metta Sama, Ginger Hendricks, Amy Knox Brown, Penelope Niven, Pamela Uschuk, Annette Allen, Emily Herring Wilson, and everyone at the Center for Women Writers; Brit Kaufman and all the good folks at Carolina Mountains festival; Katrina Denza, Hope Williams, and everyone at Weymouth Center for the Arts & Humanities; the generous people at Wildacres, to name only a few. To the literary journals that have published my work (listed in the front of this book) and their tireless, generous, mostly volunteer staff: deepest appreciation. To scores of writers, far too many to name, with whom I've become friends in the global writing community: I hope I've expressed my gratitude to you along the way.

I can't begin to thank all my friends from home: Melissa Shrewsbury, Lora Myers Call, and Melissa Nelson, friends from childhood and always; neighbors, past and present; classmates from North Wilkes High, Salem College, and Queens University of Charlotte; Salem College students with bright writing futures of their own; coworkers and friends in the community at Wake Health, Salem College, Wilkes Community College, Surry Community College, Wilkes Regional Public Library, Cultural Arts Council of Wilkes, Yadkin Arts Council, Wilkes Reads Together, and countless others. Thank you.

To early readers and reviewers who were generous enough to offer kind endorsements: Sara Pritchard, Renée Nicholson, Ron Rash, Robert Morgan, Pinckney Benedict, Kim Church, and Charles Dodd White. Your words I treasure.

Thanks as well to the entire staff at West Virginia University Press, especially Derek Krissoff, Abby Freeland, Jason Gosnell, Than Saffel, Sarah Munroe, and Rachel King for believing in this book and pouring your hearts and minds into making it better.

Finally, boundless thanks to the maker.

Burning Slag

All the children had been given away, and now Darcus Mullins found herself driving the curving road up toward Isaban to look again at the burning slag heap. Along the way, she would pass the house where Leonard had been sent, and she would slow the car to a crawl so she could peer down into Hatfield Bottom where he sat playing in the mud with his new foster sisters, patting pies into shape and drying them on the low stone flood wall. Between the leafless trees she could see his dark head bent in concentration, the little white heads of his new sisters beside him, the littler one with her arm crooked up over his neck.

The screen door to the little clapboard house was scotched open, and Darcus knew that the girls' mother was keeping a careful eye on the children. The windows were rolled down in the car, and Darcus heard music coming from the house, Donna Fargo. "Funny Face."

Darcus inched down the mountain, taking a long slow view of the swing set next to the house and the coal shed nearby, piled near full. There was a pony in the pasture between the house and the trailer where old Eudora Hatfield the landowner lived, that looked like maybe it belonged to the blond-haired foster family. On a previous drive-by, Darcus had noticed the rabbit hutch where the girls had seemed to be showing Leonard how to hold one of the animals without getting scratched.

If she had had a man who'd built a rabbit hutch, Darcus had thought sullenly, well, then that would've been a different story.

She eased the car quietly around the mountain road until she reached the dirt drive leading into the foster family's yard. There was a moment when she considered why she was there. Then Leonard's eyes caught sight of her and just as before, she gunned the old Plymouth, its corroded muffler detonating charges that rang off the sheer rock–faced mountains around them. *Dat! Dat! Dat!* Again, as before, Leonard lit to his feet like a deer, head perched high on his neck, arms akimbo, and this time, mud pies falling to the rain-soaked earth below. Set running by his heart, nothing more, he chased the car, tears streaming to his ears, bare feet slapping in the slick bottom, the knees of his high-waters soaked through.

The little tow-headed girls stood yelling for him. "*Lin-*nard!" they cried. "*Lin-n*ard!" Alerting their mother who came out the door and down the porch steps, eight months pregnant, wearing a smock-top that couldn't be worn for much longer, and watching as Darcus's car rounded the mountain, coming in view now of the backside of the house.

Darcus glanced over the edge of the steep road into the narrow backyard at a couple of pawpaw trees, the leaves of which had gone bright yellow, the few lingering fruit black. Through the rearview she saw Leonard doubled over bawling, now running again, and then finally just staring as she drove out of sight.

She was a heartless woman, the pregnant mother must've thought as she stroked Leonard's wet face and drew him up under one arm to kiss his head. But what did she know about it?

* * *

When she reached Isaban, Darcus stopped the car by an old shack bearing metal signs advertising Dental Snuff and Spark Plug chewing tobacco. She smelled the oily smoke of the slag heap before she saw it smoldering in the distance. She had grown up by such a slag heap as this, and now she wanted to remember it. She saw her daddy climbing out of the bed of the truck he paid the driver a quarter a day to ride home in, a dollar symbol painted on the vehicle's doors to indicate the driver was for hire. He would smile when he saw her and a strike of white would slash across his blackened face. They lived in the foreign section of the camp with the Italians, though they were not Italian. "Portyghee" is what her mommy said they were, but that's not what others called them. They lived near the burning gob pile that kept her poor mother scrubbing away at the oily residue that coated the plaster walls of their house.

Darcus lit a cigarette and wondered how it was she hadn't been sent away to the penitentiary. The judge had found her guilty by reason of temporary insanity, taken her children, and let her go. Sonny's family had snatched up the kids, divvying them up among themselves before she'd even been released from the psych ward in Bluewell. The littler ones would've already forgotten her by now. One or two were up in Virginia or down in North Carolina, but Leonard was here and he would remember.

It was the kerosene burns on the babies what found her negligent, sores where they'd crawled through raw fuel that one of the older ones had sloshed when filling the heater. Most people said she'd lost her sense from being beaten so often in the head, but they showed no pity on her. Now here she was, wandering the hillsides like a revenant.

* * *

Leonard had been her brightest and best-behaved child, and she knew he would not cause any trouble that would make the foster family send him packing. He would not steal, as two of her others were liable to do. The eight months pregnant foster mother would never let go of Darcus's boy. And so it was up to Darcus to draw him back herself. She was not so off in the head she didn't want someone to love her, and Leonard loved her more than all the rest combined. It had been Leonard who'd stood up to his old man whenever he'd taken to thumping on Darcus. Leonard balling up his small fists and issuing threats that only got him his own set of bruises to match his mother's. The boy had been too small, but his love was plenty big enough to save Darcus from the hollow feeling that haunted her day and night now that the old bastard was dead. "Leonard," she murmured in the car. "My baby."

* * *

The rabbits kicked inside the gunnysack until their bodies righted themselves into some measure of comfort. One was dyed yellow, the other pink, for Easter, though both showed patches of white where the dye had begun to fade. Darcus put the sack in the floorboard behind her seat and sped away in the old Plymouth, the car's usual backfires going unnoticed today, as the children were in school and the eight months pregnant foster mother was off taking her cosmetology examination so she could open her own beauty shop in the little mobile-home trailer her husband had dragged into the bottom and underpinned with thin sheet metal designed to look like cinder blocks. Darcus had taken a turn around the little trailer, climbing up to peer inside the screened windows at the white Congoleum floors and the fancy mirrored walls. If she'd had a man who'd bought her a trailer, it would be a different story indeed.

But Darcus's man was dead, and she'd killed him, and what she now had was two rabbits that had not long before been handled by her baby boy Leonard. She wanted something soft to hold against her cheek, something smelling of her Leonard perhaps, and so she toted the rabbits up around the bend and sat with them in her lap in the long front seat of the Plymouth. She stroked the rabbits' soft fur as she stared into the burning slag heap. Its glowing embers had always had a calming effect on Darcus no matter how hard her mother had tried to scare her with threats of the devil coming to get her if she didn't quit misbehaving. If she didn't quit letting boys put hickies on her titties. She recalled the way her mother had clasped her jaw and craned it side to side to have a better look at her neck. "You ain't careful," her mother warned, "your whoring around is going to saddle you up with a whole slew of young ones." And she was right. Darcus was even then pregnant with her first, although that wasn't counting the one that had slipped out and fallen into the outhouse pit. But that one had been dead, Darcus was sure. She'd stared into the slurry after it and when no sound of a baby's cry came, she was satisfied it was so and went on about her business, though with a sadness she hadn't known before. Imogene, she called that one.

Darcus opened the door of the Plymouth and climbed out, nuzzling the yellow rabbit to her face and closing her eyes as she delighted in the silky fleece of the animal's fur against her skin. "So soft," she said, bending and lowering the rabbit onto the steaming earth. The rabbit leapt forward and cried out as its feet were set ablaze by the burning embers, hopping wildly now deeper and deeper into the burning culm. Darcus stood watching, a distant expression on her face, as the animal soon fell over dead and burned to a cinder.

* * *

The school bus was letting the children off at the foster family's house when Darcus rounded the curve coming into Hatfield Bottom. There was Leonard holding hands with his foster sisters as they crossed the road, a little chain of paper dolls. The eight months pregnant foster mother stood waiting at the screen door. Darcus rolled down the window and called Leonard's name. The boy turned, and Darcus held up the pink and white rabbit.

"Flopsy!" cried the smaller of the two tow-headed girls.

The eight months pregnant mother came down the steps of the porch with a look of panic on her face.

"I was just going up to the park to let Flopsy play in the grass," Darcus said.

The eight months pregnant mother broke into a run. On the stereo behind her, Donna Fargo sang, "I'm the happiest girl in the whole USA."

The smallest of the little blond-haired girls wrenched her hand free from Leonard's grip and sped toward the Plymouth.

The eight months pregnant mother stumbled and cried out. "Leonard!" she called.

Darcus opened the car door. "Come on, baby," she said. "We'll all go."

Robbing Pillars

Maiden Estep leads the Red Hat into Number Six at Beartown, where the mine starts. They walk at first, back to the crawl, miles deep inside, under the town of Grundy. Already, they have cut a strip in both directions, and soon they'll be coming back through the middle, robbing pillars it's called, the most danger any of them have been exposed to except the old guys, the robbing line, and the dynamite guys. Maiden runs the scoop, loading what they dig and blast loose onto the conveyor that carries it out through the mountain and into the yard. A couple times a night, he climbs off the scoop and crawls along the belt, throwing pieces back on that have fallen over, up and down the narrow gangway.

The Red Hat's name is Charlie Hawkins, barely out of high school. Most of the men know him already. Got a little girl pregnant his junior year. Who hadn't gotten a little girl pregnant at some point?

The kid's tall, six five or six, thereabouts, and carries it all through the legs, not the trunk of his body as some men do.

From the knee to his hip, he is nearly as tall as the mine is deep in this section, so the crawl behind Maiden is cumbersome.

"Don't bow your back," Maiden warns. "4160 running overhead."

Maiden is only a White Hat himself. This is the first time he's been part of robbing pillars, and he is uneasy, even though the actual pillar robbing is not his job. Once they've humped out the vein they're working on, the robbers will come behind and start pulling the pillars, the mountain collapsing at their heels.

There is water standing in ruts along the crawl, which dampens the knees of their work pants. Occasionally they hear a drip, but once they travel deeper inside, the floor of the shaft becomes dry again. Visibility is only possible by the dim lights of their miners' caps, powered by wet-cell batteries. Overhead, the 4160 hums in Maiden's ears.

The only other thing so far that has spooked him is the blasting. When the dynamite men come in, the others hunker down where they are and protect themselves as best they can. The only real thing between them and fire in the hole is prayer. Not even the unbelievers chance it. "Faith can move mountains," the miners say. "Just pray like hell it don't have to."

A case of the nerves makes the Red Hat natter on about something or other behind Maiden. Baseball. Goose Gossage. Maiden has never watched a game of professional baseball or any other sport, on television or anywhere else, but he can't imagine pulling for a player from New York City. He likes only Westerns and war movies, though he doesn't mention it to the Red Hat. Maiden lets him blather on, respectfully saying nothing, only occasionally issuing a calm reminder now and again about the current running overhead.

The Red Hat is having trouble, though, and somewhere deep in the pit of Maiden's stomach he knows something's going to happen. Something bad. It's as if a ghost has suddenly whispered in his ear. His flesh crawls all over and he throws another piece of slab up onto the conveyor. Then he turns to look at the Red Hat, low-crawling for every penny he's worth. Maiden thinks of learning to low-crawl himself at the boy's age, nineteen or thereabouts, in the army, basic training, under concertino wire, fake rounds fired overheard and only sporadically. Nothing nearly so dangerous at 4160. The Red Hat hasn't thrown the first chunk of coal up onto the belt, but Maiden does not reprimand. The boy is scared. Maiden lets him prattle on.

"Got an aunt over here in Grundy," the kid says. "Reckon we might be up under her house?"

Maiden doesn't answer. Says only again, "Watch it there now."

"Hard to say, I guess. Never know though. Could be we are. Right up under Jimmy's old room. Jimmy's gone off to Beckley. We got people there. Know anybody in Beckley? I knew this one girl from War, nearby you know, and buddy I'm telling you she was abou—"

And then, just like that, Maiden sees things happen twice before his eyes. One version takes place quick. In an instant, he sees the Red Hat stretch forward with one arm, his head buried into the earth. Then he bows up for leverage to push off again. And as he pitches back on one knee, he arches his spine and the wet strap of his mining belt draws too near the 4160 and sparks. "Oh, Lord!" the boy cries. "Oh, Lord! Oh, Lord! Oh, Lord! Oh, Lord!" Over and over and over while Maiden screams back down through the shaft that a man has gotten tangled up in the wire. "Kill the switch!" Maiden screams. "Cut the goddamn juice! A man's hit! A man's hit! Good, Jesus, a man's hit!"

"Oh, Lord! Oh, Lord! Oh, Lord!" the Red Hat seems to say, even though he is a puddle of flesh, melting like cheese but smelling of meat. Maiden knows he's dead, but the kid keeps talking and Maiden just lies there, waiting helplessly as he was taught to do in miners' school. He does not extend a hand. He doesn't rush to the boy's side, though the urge to is overpowering and Maiden screams his guts out and cries for God in heaven to have mercy. He's just a kid. Nineteen. Twenty at most. A big, gangly legged kid whose kneecaps have been blown off. "Jesus! Oh, Jesus! Hurry the fuck up down there!" Maiden calls again and again before the power is thrown and the Red Hat stops chattering.

* * *

In the other version, Maiden had seen a ghost behind the Red Hat. Some kind of phantom. A wisp or something. It was blurry but distinct enough that Maiden had fixed his gaze upon it while the kid had talked on and on about his cousin Jimmy going off to Beckley.

Maiden's wife begs him every night to quit. Number Six is about to shut down soon anyway, she tells him. When Maiden dons his carbide light and packs his dinner bucket with water and leftovers, she resorts to threats, name-calling. "Maiden, you son of a bitch! Maiden! Maiden!" He lets her speak her piece. Goes on to work. Someone has to run the scoop.

Today they are coming back up the middle, robbing all the pillars. Number Six will chase them tunnel by tunnel as they pull timbers and wait for the roof to collapse one room at a time so they can mine the fall. That's money standing there, supporting the roof, and the company wants every square inch.

The Red Hat is not the first man Maiden has known who has died, nor the only death he's witnessed firsthand. Jenkins Cline was caught between two cars on the tipple of a breaker. Clarence Price was killed by a rush of slush when water forced it out the gangway. Julius Reed was tamping a hole when powder in the tunnel exploded. During miners' training, Maiden heard about men suffocating when they walked into pockets of gas, being struck by frozen slags of culm, or being smothered by a rush of dirt working at the culm bank. Men had been run over by loaders, crushed by cave-ins when ribs gave way. They'd been burned, mangled by machinery, and electrocuted like Charlie, the young Red Hat.

When Maiden runs the scoop back through the shaft where the boy died, he wonders about the aunt's house in Grundy and whether or not they had indeed been somewhere under it when the kid had gotten caught up in the wire. It's risky, thinking about the dead so soon, if old wives' tales are to be believed. Bad luck. Better if he thinks of something else, just in case, but the Red Hat consumes his thoughts. Goose What-was-his-name? And then the boy melting like a Popsicle before him. He wonders where the boy's aunt might've been standing. Had she felt something, deep in the earth, some pull on her like a dowsing stick drawn by a vein of ground water?

The robbers begin taking out a few of the timbers as Maiden waits near the other room with the scoop and watches. Those remaining start to buckle under the weight of the roof, but the process isn't as fast as he expects. The roof does not cave in immediately in order for them to load the fallen coal onto Maiden's scoop and send it out into the yard. The robbers go one timber at a time, striking with their hammers, prying and shoving on each one until it kicks loose from the floor and the weight of the rock above their heads is redistributed to the others still standing. It's a game of Russian roulette, no telling when the roof will fall, so they work slowly, pulling one timber and then watching, listening as the other supports begin to splinter and crack in the dark around them. There is nervous energy between the robbers. They talk casually together, laugh loudly, estimating if they should maybe pull another one. Watching by the dim torch of his carbide light becomes unbearable for Maiden. He can feel the weight pressing down on them, inch by inch, timbers slowly splintering and buckling all around, but still the roof is content to hold.

"Son of a bitch," one of the robbers says. "She ain't budging. Run the scoop up here, hoss, and let's see if we can shake this bitch loose."

Maiden realizes he is being addressed, but still he hesitates. "What's that?"

"Run the scoop this a'way and see if it don't shake the ground just enough."

All four of the men, including Maiden, are working on their stomachs. Whenever the roof does decide to fall, they won't be able to run. The robbers can't risk pulling out another timber. Maiden watches as they make their way toward him to the other room, a safe distance from the shattering timbers. At least he has the scoop, which might be fast enough.

He wedges himself into the machine and drives forward cautiously as the robbers tell him how to proceed.

"Tap on that one right there," says Arbury Massey. "Easy ought to do it, and then hightail it back."

Goose Gossage was the ball player's name, Maiden remembers. And then he is caught by a feeling of being drawn upward. He hears a low growl of thunder and looks around to see that the cap boards have begun to twist and rip. The watery contents of his stomach seem to rise like a wave. But it's not only that; the blood in his heart and veins pools at the top of his head.

The Red Hat's aunt is standing directly over him, he realizes. Maiden closes his eyelids, lifts his face, and as the tears well in his eyes, they too are drawn up in streaks that wash the coal dust from his temples and over his forehead. The woman kneels to the floor and places her hand, just there, on his cheek. And then the earth rains down.

The Immortal Jesse James

The closer they get to Stanton, Missouri, the more often they see signs advertising Meramec Caverns. Billboards and barn roofs announcing JESSE JAMES'S HIDEOUT! UNDERGROUND MARVELS JUST AHEAD!

"Who wants to go?" Boy Baby asks democratically, speaking over his shoulder to his younger brothers, Melvin and Billy, in the backseat. He calls them Hummer and Billy the Kid, or Hummer and Wild Bill, or various other famous Billies that strike him at the time. He likes nicknames. His older brother Parmeleigh conferred the name Boy Baby upon him, and he'd liked that, called it his Indian name. "You, Running Bear. Me, Boy Baby," he joked.

He ignores Jane, who is holding a hand on their four-month-old daughter riding on the front seat between them in Boy's '62 Catalina. Jane is still scowling about the car breaking down near St. Clair. He'd snapped a timing chain drag racing a sweet little '67 Super Sport. He'd kept up with it until then, though. It had taken him nearly two hours to walk into town for the parts and back, and then another three to take off the fan and the water pump and the housing surrounding the timing chain. He opened up an old scab on his knuckles from a previous repair, but he'd fixed the car.

And still she is pissed. "We just got back on the highway, Reuben," she says, exasperated. She calls him Reuben.

They are traveling Route 66, the Mother Road, toward Rialto, California, where they will stay with her sister Mary Polly for a while until they find their own place, Boy Baby says. He and his brothers are caught spellbound by every billboard promising strange and wondrous sights. Boy has filled their heads with visions of painted deserts and petrified forests, of wigwam motels and red rock canyons. This is why he has brought them along, he reminds her, to show them some little bit of the world, even parts unknown to him.

"It'll be fun, puss," he says. "We'll camp."

They have been *camping* since they left Gary, Indiana, sleeping in the car at truck stops or on concrete picnic tables at roadside rests. It's the middle of July, and even at night the temperature hovers near seventy. Jane is exhausted, and she and the baby are covered in road grime. Black sweat bands have formed in the creases of the infant's pudgy arms and legs. They have been bathing at campsites or washing up in public bathrooms, but the wind through the open windows keeps her hair feeling oily and her skin feeling tight and dirty. She pulls out the diaper bag and goes to work lifting little rolls of baby fat and smearing away dirt with a burp cloth dampened with baby oil.

Melvin and Billy are in agreement. They want to see Jesse James's hideout, too. They are romping and roughhousing in the big backseat of the Catalina. They look like separate miniature versions of Boy Baby, Melvin sharing Boy's dark complexion and Billy taking the same beefy build, which makes him seem older than Melvin, though he isn't.

"I told Mary Polly we'd be there in a couple days," Jane

says, changing the baby's diaper on the vinyl seat of the Pontiac as it sails down the road.

"Ah, puss. What's your hurry?"

They'd run into thunderstorms the night before, which had unnerved Jane so badly that Boy had relented and pulled over to sleep at a truck stop outside St. Louis. He generally prefers driving at night, can make better time, he says, time better spent seeing the sights after a little predawn shut-eye. But it wasn't only the storm. She feels jumpier now that the baby is with them.

He needed to take a leak anyway, he said. Melvin and Billy had already conked out, so the only fun he could possibly have was rolling down the window and letting the rain blow in on them. The wipers were barely able to beat the rain away fast enough, though, so Jane wasn't up for anymore fooling. "For God's sake, Reuben," she said, and he let it rest.

Once they were inside the truck stop, she went to work making fresh bottles for the baby and storing as many as she could carry in the diaper bag. Boy Baby wouldn't want to stop once they were making good time again. Unless, of course, there was something interesting to see, a giant bottle of ketchup, say, or a teepee selling fireworks.

She bathed the baby in the restroom sink and smeared Baby Magic lotion over her corpulent little body and wrestled her into her pajamas. She brushed the baby's fine hair and twirled it around her finger so that it made one lustrous curl on her head. The rain had let up some, and when she came out of the bathroom, she found Boy Baby playing cards with Melvin and Billy at one of the booths near the windows.

They were playing with the deck of cards Boy was almost court martialed over. Melvin and Billy know the story, too.

Boy was marching through the jungle when the lieutenant—sometimes it's a sergeant—decided they were going to stop and pray for victory in battle. All the men lowered their machine guns—sometimes it's bayonets—and knelt on one knee. Boy Baby pulled out the deck of cards and spread them out on the jungle floor. The lieutenant, outraged at Boy's irreverent behavior, sent him to the rear to be locked up in the stocks for court martial. When the general asked Boy why he'd been playing cards during the battle prayer, Boy said, "This deck of cards is my Bible, your honor. The ace is the one true God. The deuce is the Father and the Son."

On the story goes, through the whole deck of cards, until someone says, "Boy, I didn't know you were in the army." He wasn't, he tells them.

And then the punch line: "I was an old gorilla fighter. I fought old gorillas."

Making her way toward the sound of Boy's voice, Jane listened to be sure they didn't order any food. There was bologna in the cooler that she intended to fry on the Coleman stove.

"The Lord giveth," Boy was saying, "and the Lord taketh away, little sons."

Billy and Melvin, who are ten and twelve respectively, did not have much to gamble with—a couple of chipped marbles and a pocket comb. But smiling triumphantly, Boy Baby reached across the table and pulled it all toward him.

Naked I came out of the womb, Jane thought, and naked shall I return.

* * *

There is an entrance fee to see the caverns, a waste of money, Jane is thinking. They already wasted too much on other stupid things like toy tomahawks and Chinese finger traps. "We have a *baby* now, Reuben. We can't stop at every tourist trap we see."

"We're not stopping at *every* tourist trap," he says, pulling into the parking lot of the Jesse James Museum in Stanton. He smiles like one of the Three Stooges and flutters his eyelashes rapidly. "Just this one." She considers poking him in the eye.

Melvin and Billy push on the back of her seat, hurry her to open the door and let them climb out. "Just a minute!" she snaps. "You're going to crush the baby." She scoops up the infant from the seat beside her and opens the door, leans forward into the dashboard, and the boys plow up out of the backseat like a couple of wild ponies. They are speed-drawing toy pistols and trying on coonskin hats in the gift shop when she and Boy Baby catch up with them.

"Buy!" they sing from across the little shop. "Look at this!" A woman with dark hair and glasses like Coke bottle bottoms is showing the boys photographs of what she claims is evidence that Jesse James was not shot and killed in 1882 as most people believe.

"This picture is of Jesse James's ear in 1880-something," she says, pointing to a framed black-and-white photograph displayed above shelves of sundry tourist-trap knickknacks. "Probably shortly before his *supposed* death in 1882." She points to another photo. "And this one, taken in 1950, shows the ear of J. Frank Dalton, the alias Jesse assumed after he faked his death and escaped to South America."

"They're identical!" Melvin says.

The woman goes on with her spiel. "As further proof, Jesse James was shot twice in the chest during the Civil War, leaving him with scars in the exact same locations as two scars on J. Frank Dalton's chest."

Apparently, J. Frank Dalton had come out of hiding on his hundredth birthday, reclaiming his name and notoriety before his death in 1952. He had returned to visit the area—and also to promote the caverns and museum for a time. The proprietress claims to have seen the scars herself. She doesn't care what anyone says. Jesse James had lived to be an old man, and she had met him.

"They have wax figures inside," Billy says, swinging on Boy Baby's brown arm. "And the barber chair where he got his last haircut."

"How much to see the hideout?" Boy asks the woman.

"Hideout's up the road," she says. "This here is the museum."

Boy turns and looks at Jane and the kids, then back at the woman. "How far?" he asks.

"Couple miles," the woman says.

"Would you rather go in here, or have a look at his hideout up the road?" Jane asks the boys, trying to feign excitement as she switches the baby from one hip to the other.

"But they got wax figures," they say again to Boy.

"What say we hop in the car and head on up to the hideout, Hummer?" Boy says, wiping the coonskin cap off Melvin's head and putting it back on the shelf. "What do you think there, Billy Boy?"

They are none too happy to leave the museum without seeing the wax likenesses of Jesse and the other outlaws. But they leave the cap guns on the counter and mope outside in the direction of the car.

"Hope you ain't afraid of bats," Melvin grumbles from the backseat, folding his arms across his chest.

Jane cuts a sharp eye at Boy Baby, who climbs in behind the steering wheel, carefree as a tumbleweed.

"There ain't no bats, puss," he says, smiling. "They're just trying to scare you."

But there are bats, and she knows it. He's lying to her, but somewhere deep inside she also knows that he is impervious to any real danger, try as he might to meet it head-on. And as long as she's with him, so is she. He's always trying to show them something, though she's never sure what exactly. They left Indiana with a tank of gas and their pockets turned inside out. "How are we going to get all the way to California on one tank of gas?" she wanted to know.

"Maybe we don't get all the way," he said. "Maybe we get as far as Oklahoma. You ever been to Oklahoma, puss?"

* * *

He cradles the baby in one arm and pulls Jane close with the other as they walk toward the entrance of Meramec Caverns. "I got you," he says.

They descend into the first dank crater beneath the earth, a tour guide motioning the group to follow him onto a gangway winding a path down around a log cabin, of all things. It's strange seeing a cabin down there, Jane thinks, which looks so small inside the cavernous chamber. It reminds her of a song Boy likes her to sing, "Build Me a Cabin in Gloryland."

Colored lights illuminate the perimeter of the cavern, blues and purples and pinks. The whole thing is lurid and artificial, like a dream, not at all like heaven. If anything, it's more like hell, she thinks, a little cabin in the corner of hell itself.

Still, she wants to see inside. She imagines finding the cabin somewhere along their journey, setting up her little Coleman stove on whatever rickety old table awaits inside, frying strips of bacon while Melvin and Billy erect a house with Boy's playing cards.

There is a neon sign above the cabin: MERAMAC CAVERNS. JESSE JAMES'S HIDEOUT. They are at the back of the group, craning their necks and squinting for a better view. Why would someone go to the trouble of building a cabin inside a cave? Jane wonders. Jesse James doesn't strike her as the kind of man looking for permanence. The cabin had belonged to an obscure moonshiner, the guide tells them, but Jane fails to see the connection. Why has it been brought into the cave? And why is there a sign over it suggesting it has anything to do with Jesse James?

When the car had broken down, Boy Baby had taken Melvin with him, leaving Jane alone with the infant and the younger of the two boys. There had been moments when she wondered if he would return, not because she feared he'd ever abandon them, but because it was likely that he'd gotten distracted by something he wanted to see or do. She tried to imagine the strip of highway from where they sat stranded alongside the road to St. Clair. Was there anything that might lure him away from his mission? A fruit stand selling cherries and watermelons? A hotrod? A mountain or stream like something out of a movie?

Behind the tour guide and all around, shadowy images begin to take shape: giant stalagmites which "grow," they are told, from the ceiling, and equally large stone spikes called stalactites that spear up treacherously from the floor. It reminds Jane of some kind of trap. As if the earth above and below them will suddenly snap shut and gore them all to death. She never imagined so much architecture was inside a cave. She's never thought much about caves at all. But if she had, she might've guessed that they were empty earthen rooms like those she's seen in Westerns. Homey almost, swept clean, with the ashes of long ago campfires neatly circled by smooth river rocks and outfitted with torches one could light upon entering.

She takes the baby from Boy's arm and clutches her close.

"Come along," the guide says, and they wind their way through crevices and strangely illuminated passageways of striated rock formations. Water drips constantly, but it's hard to tell from which direction. Their voices echo round and away down the corridors behind and in front of them. It's like a house of mirrors, she thinks, a fun house, they call them, though she's not sure why. A person could very easily get lost in there.

"Imagine," the guide says now. "None of this might ever have been discovered if Lewis and Clark had not bravely headed west into unknown territories."

He explains how the caverns were formed by streams that eroded the land over millions of years. It looks to Jane like a church, a big Catholic church with walls of melted wax. He speaks of Pre-Columbian Native Americans who likely used the caverns. Missouri is the cave state, he reminds them, as he points out Indian hieroglyphics: stick figures on horses hunting deer and buffalo, others fishing with spears.

"Limestone caves like this one are often wet. Some have underground lakes or rivers," he tells them. "Perfect for campsites and watering holes, but not a very good permanent shelter. Unless you're a bat," he adds.

Jane tenses at the mention of bats and pulls the blanket down over the baby. It's too cold down here, she thinks, hoping the baby won't catch sick, praying they don't see bats.

"Not to worry, though," the old man continues. "The eastern pipistrelle is harmless. She's only interested in finding a place to roost with her babies. Males roost alone during summer months but will rejoin the females again when it's time to reproduce."

Typical, Jane thinks.

Melvin and Billy are bored with talk of the mating habits of bats and begin shoving each other as if they are going to throw the other over the steep side of the pathway into the abyss below.

"The convoluted twists and turns of caverns have made them popular dwellings for outlaws looking to lay low," the guide says, and both boys straighten up again to listen. "A cave's walls are impenetrable, offering no greater protection. And total darkness," the old man says, "hides many secrets."

They shuffle along behind the crowd as it picks its way through the labyrinthine tunnels to an underground river. The baby has fallen asleep and the boys, too, now seem lulled by the cool darkness and the rhythmic sounds of dripping water. The baby yawns and Jane is made to yawn now too.

Boy Baby tosses something from his pocket into Jane's hair and yells, "Bat!"

She jerks and swats her hair and screams for Boy to "*get it out*" though she knows as soon as she flinches that he's played a prank on her. But now the baby is crying and if Jane had a gun, she'd shoot him dead. "You idiot!" she hisses. She untangles the pocket comb he won from Melvin from her hair and throws it at him.

"It was just a joke," he says, grinning too wide, trying to make up. "Come here, puss."

The baby is squalling and people turn with angry looks for her to make it be quiet. The guide is finally talking about Jesse James, and they want to hear it.

"Jesse James was a Confederate soldier," the guide says, raising his voice to drown the cries of the baby. "One of Quantrill's Raiders. Along with his brother Frank, and of course Cole and James Younger."

Jane bounces the baby as they stand in place, waiting for the old fart to finish the story and move on again. "It's okay," she coos. "Mommy's got you."

"Oh my, but they were a ruthless lot." The old guide is a good storyteller. The baby has hushed a little, and now he has them, so he takes his time. "Legend has it that when Quantrill found out that Union soldiers were milling the saltpeter here in the caverns for munitions, he decided to blow the whole operation to kingdom come."

Boy Baby pulls a Chinese finger trap from his pocket. "I'm sorry," he whispers to Jane. "Cuff me and lock me up."

Jane rolls her eyes and tightens the blanket around the baby, gives another impatient bounce.

"And he and his men did just that. But later, you see, he remembered the place and brought his gang of outlaws down here to hide. They'd robbed a train in Arkansas called the Little Rock Express. Many, many years later, the owner of Meramac Caverns found a chamber that we now refer to as Loot Rock. No one even knew it existed. Inside that chamber, he found the coffers taken from the Little Rock Express all those years ago, and a large cache of rifles and shackles."

"Can we go there?" a kid near the front of the group asks. "Will you take us to Loot Rock?"

Boy Baby, trying to escape the bamboo finger trap, looks up at the mention of Loot Rock.

"Too dangerous, I'm afraid," the old man says. "The river's too high right now. It's only accessible when the water is much lower. That's how it was discovered. Mr. Dill, the owner, saw a gap under one of the walls, and beneath the wall, he noticed that the river flowed under it. He looked closer, and that's when he found the artifacts."

Boy studies the underground river, which is cordoned off from the dimly lit path. Jane knows he's imagining what it must have been like to be an outlaw, thinking to himself that he could swim that river and cross under the wall to Loot Rock if he wanted. She knows he could do it, too. In another life, he could've been an outlaw, she thinks. She looks at him, and he tries again to make her smile and forgive him. He wrestles in mock futility with the finger trap. He pulls and the trap tightens further, pinching into the flesh around his battered knuckles. She wonders if he would trade lives for the chance to rob a train and outrun an angry posse.

They follow the crowd into the final chamber where rows

of plastic chairs are lined up theatre style. Jane gladly takes a seat and plops the baby's diaper bag in another one next to her. The tour guide flips a switch and colored lights flash on a beautiful wall of what he calls "flowstones." It's the grand finale. Boy and the kids sit, too, and an old recording of "God Bless America" blares from speakers mounted in plain view around the chamber. The baby looks around at the colored lights but does not cry.

"Help me," Boy says. "I'm twapped."

But he hasn't been pardoned yet. Jane repositions the baby in one arm and takes his hand with her other. He frees himself, rests his arm in her lap. She runs her thumb over the bridge of his scarred knuckles and perches her head on his shoulder.

Barry Gibb
Is the Cutest Bee Gee

The lawn chairs are still cold when we carry our stuff out at ten sharp. I carry a blanket, sunglasses, a hat, a towel for each of us, and an armload of homework on my first trip. Mama has her baby oil and iodine, a cup of coffee, and her cigarette case. She's wearing a white terrycloth strapless jumper she will peel off when she's ready, and flip-flops.

Mama aligns her chair with the sun and adjusts both ends the way she wants: feet down, back up so she can peer out over the subdivision while she sips her coffee and enjoys her first cigarette. Then she lays the chair flat, spreads a towel over it, and strips down. A thin white scar peeks out of her bikini, but her stomach is flat and her waist is T-tiny. I wear my blue track shorts until Mama makes me take them off. But I refuse to wear a two-piece. "Your belly is going to be white as a fish," she says, and I think, More like a whale, you mean.

She will finish her cigarette before I get everything in order to suit me, my blanket spread out in case I feel the urge to reposition. I carry out a bag of chips and Little Debbie cakes, even though Mama cautions that girls can't eat this way forever. I raise the window in the kitchen and find a station we like on the radio, turn the volume up, pour a glass of tea, and refill the ice trays. "Want a pop?" I ask. But she doesn't. "Anything else?"

"Not right now," she says.

I see her through the kitchen window, rubbing down her legs and arms, the fiery red ember of a Winston as she takes a hard drag, and I remember suntan lotion, go back for it because I cannot stand oil of any kind. I don't like getting my hair and suit greasy, or sticking to my chair. Mama says it's a small sacrifice. She swears by baby oil and iodine, and she ought to know. Motor oil is good, too, she says. But mayonnaise, now that will burn you good. I stick to my Coppertone 8, which I put on inside the house where it's warm, hoping it will soak in before I hit the cool air outside. Mama says I shouldn't even bother if I'm going to wear sunscreen, but I worry about ultraviolet rays.

"Sun's good for you," she says. "Clear up that acne." I have this gross crater on my forehead, so I'm willing to listen even though I don't act like it.

I bring the bottle with me and circle around Mama so she can do my back. I will have to do hers, too, so I grab a wet washrag to wipe Mama's oil from my hands afterward. I don't want to get the pages of my library books greasy.

By 10:15, I am unfolding my chair. I always leave the newer one for Mama, take the one with the busted strap. One of the gears is broken, too, so I have to lie flat on my back. I get everything the way I want and then lie down. "What time is it?" I ask, and Mama checks her watch latched around the frame of her chair.

"10:20," she says.

"That's all? God, I'm dying."

"You'll live," Mama says, crushing out her cigarette in the grass.

"Want an oatmeal cake?" I ask. She doesn't, but I do and then I want milk, too, so I go inside for a glass and bring back the coffee pot to refill her cup while I'm at it. I have two cakes and pin the wrappers under a book so they won't blow away. The sun feels good, but the wind breaks chill bumps all over me. I wonder why it is that we look so white out here, during the day. Even Mama. In the evening, in our shorts, we look dark already. Mama mostly, but I do, too. "Brown as biscuits," Daddy used to say. "Little Hot-Rize Southern biscuits. Nummy nummy nummy," as he nuzzled his chin behind Mama's ear and pressed his body up behind hers in a way that made me happy and grossed me out.

He's probably at church looking all saintly right now, like everyone in our neighborhood. It is Sunday morning, but Mama and I don't give a whit about going to church. "We're pagans," I tell her. "You know, like the Mayans." She knows who the Mayans are because we saw an episode on *That's Incredible!* about human sacrifice. That's where I got the idea for my paper, my last assignment. After that, school is out for two months.

The sun passes behind a cloud and stays there until every bit of heat escapes my skin. I hold my hand over my leg, check for my shadow. "Too cloudy," I say, shivering. "Look."

She doesn't bother, but she knows what I'm talking about. "It's there," she says. "Just can't see it."

I look again but see nothing. "What's the temperature supposed to be?"

"Ninety-four."

"Wonder what it is now?"

"M mmm'm mmmm," she says. She is clearing her mind of every earthly affair.

"Feels cold," I say.

"Hush," Mama says.

"Got to pee. Need anything?"

"Mm mmm." She grunts this time.

I go inside, let the screen door slap, and feel Mama cracking open an eye at me in frustration.

"Mesoamericans built pyramids," I recite from my book, "such as the Pyramid of the Sun, located in San Juan, Mexico, the place where men became gods."

On my return to Mama and the sun, I make a quick pass through the kitchen to scrounge around for something else to munch on. There's leftover bacon and canned biscuits under a paper towel, so I make up two and carry them out. "Want one?" I ask and this time Mama takes one and sits up.

"You drinking that tea?" she asks.

I hand it over and we share sips between bites. Now the sun is out again and higher in the sky, inching its way through its orbital path.

"Ready to flip?" I ask.

"Sun just came out."

"I'm dy-ing," I groan, my vision still blooming into purple halos from staring into the sun and then walking into the dark cave of the house. I wonder whether I can go another hour and flip anyway.

"What about this, Mama?" I ask. "'Indian priests read the stars like we might read a tabloid predicting the end of time.' No," I say, striking the sentence. "Maybe this: 'People in the ancient world believed the sun had lived and died many times, always to be replaced by a new sun identical to the one before it.'" I like the way I sound in papers, a different me.

I gaze out over the adjacent backyards, which are strewn with bicycles and blow-up kiddie pools and old croquet sets I've never seen anyone using. The other neighborhood tanners won't be out for another hour. Mama and I are always outside way before anyone else. Kimberly's mom is the darkest person in the neighborhood, but she gets most of her sun at the country club, where she is learning to play tennis with her married supervisor from R.J. Reynolds.

Kimberly is my best friend. We play jacks on her cool kitchen floor to keep out of the heat. She plays better than anyone I know. She can do her sets without touching another jack, even when they're stacked. She can do her elevens or nines, even when they're spread halfway across the kitchen. She has a nice way of skimming her hand over the surface of the linoleum, too, very lightly. It's all about timing. And practice.

"Did you know," she told me once, studying one of the jacks as she held it up between her fingers, "that armies use these to maim their enemies?"

I shook my head.

"My uncle told me."

"Which one?" I hoped it wasn't Tim.

"Donnie," she said. "Only instead of jack rocks, they're called Punji sticks and they're dipped in poison or smeared with poop, so whoever steps on them will get gangrene and die."

"Eww, that's gross."

"I know."

If we're not playing jacks, we're choreographing dances like those we watch on *Solid Gold*. I am not a natural like Kimberly, but I do take after Mama and can usually get the steps down pretty fast. With the strobe lights going, we look like we're being struck by lightning. We are brown as Indians. Our teeth are white as stars. The rhythm of the music pulses in our temples, our hearts, and we feel our blood gushing around inside us like twin volcanoes.

On Sundays like today, not another soul is in the neighborhood until Kimberly's uncles come to mow her yard. Mama is already tanned enough, but she likes to be appreciated, too, she says. And Kimberly's uncles do seem to appreciate Mama.

They come with gas cans and a cooler filled with Sun Drop and Pabst Blue Ribbon. Donnie wears mirrored sunglasses and cutoffs without a shirt. His hair is slightly longish and strawberry blond like his mustache and sideburns, and undeniably, he is the more muscular of the two. He is Mama's favorite. Aunt Jonie's, too. I imagine him walking carefully over Punji sticks in the only vision of Vietnam I can conjure, a rainy jungle tangled with kudzu, no sun, no sky in sight, signaling men behind him with hand gestures, talking without words. Hand up: stop! Hand down: careful.

I myself prefer the leaner, cleaner look of Tim whose hair is shorter but yellow as a peach like his brother's. Mama thinks Tim is too saintly looking, but she likes the way he fills out a pair of Levi's all the same, she says.

Aunt Jonie arrives with her lawn chair. She is wearing a string bikini under a little white wrap tied merely for ornamentation around her bony waist. "Girls, have I missed them?" she asks, opening her chair, sliding it next to Mama's.

"No," I say, and she grins with her tongue between her teeth and skips around all hot to trot, not like a grown woman should, I think. She considers herself the classiest, sassiest woman alive, and that's about right, I guess. Her hair is a dark brown-red, only a shade or two darker than her skin will be by the end of the summer. Her fingernails are heart-stopper crimson, she calls it, and stay looking wet like the magazines advertise.

I ask her for the thousandth time how she got her nails so long and she says, "Tabby, I'll tell you," in that tone that signals a story is coming. "Your aunt Jonie was born with fingernails this long."

Mama lifts the wet rag on her eyes and says, "With three rings on every finger and an emery board in one hand."

Aunt Jonie cackles and shoots me a clicking wink and says, "Damn straight, darling." Then she adjusts each one of her rings and stretches out on the lawn chair next to Mama.

"What time is it?" I ask. "I am burning up."

"Beauty has its price," Mama says.

I move over to the blanket spread out in the grass. It is a soft, wooly thing with reversible images on either side: a panther on one and a wolf howling at the moon on the other. It will burn me up shortly, too, but it is better than a thin sheet that would let the hard, stalky grass poke through and stab me. I open my book to a fantastic drawing of a pyramid, read the caption beneath it: "Children were ritually sacrificed in the cave wells beneath the pyramids to appease the rain god Chaac." The real pyramid, shown in the inset, looks more like a pile of rocks.

Aunt Jonie opens her cigarette case and digs out a Virginia Slims with her long nails. She spends a lot of time at a bar called Coyote Jack's, even though she is a married woman, and I suspect she dances and God knows what all with men she meets there. Now that Mama and Daddy are in a "trial separation," Mama goes to Coyote Jack's with her.

That is where she met Tam, at Coyote Jack's. "That's his name? I don't like calling a man *Tam*," I told her.

And she said, "You don't like a lot of things, Tabby." Then she said, "His name is Talmadge, if that suits you better."

He is the biggest drip that ever lived, I reminded her. "He has varicose veins on his *face*."

"Don't be ugly, Tabby," she said. "And they're not varicose veins."

She is slightly embarrassed to be going out with him, though, and anybody who knows Mama knows it. Talmadge is not Mama's kind of man. Donnie is Mama's kind of man, muscled and tan and hunky. Daddy is Mama's kind of man, dark haired, dark eyed, and deceitful. I see it all over her when he comes to pick me up on holidays. "You look good, Will," she tells him, smiling that way she does, chin down, looking up at him. And he says, "You, too, sweet thing," the heavens breaking open above him, and we both give into his charm, forget what a con he can be.

Across the way, Kimberly's uncles arrive in Donnie's battered Datsun pickup. Tim steps out of the passenger side, and my heart skips, like he is coming to pick me up for a date or something crazy like that. Mama and Aunt Jonie stop talking once they spot the men, and we all three sit there quiet in our own heads, dreaming the same dream. And what we dream is this: we dream that Donnie will woof at us and smile big and wave and say, "Hello, la-a-dies!" And Tim will laugh in spite of himself and shake his head in embarrassment and go on around to the bed of the truck and start unloading push mowers and weed eaters.

I'll imagine standing before him, waiting for him to kiss me, dying from his slowness, tortured and loving it, dying and smiling to draw him out. And what Mama and Aunt Jonie will imagine is the same, I figure, only a little grosser maybe, though I don't worry a lot about the details I know I'm surely leaving out. It's all the same thing, one dream between us, and it paralyzes us like a poison, all three of us sleeping stubbornly to a beautiful dream we want to go on forever.

"Somebody put a note in my locker," I tell Mama and Aunt Jonie after Donnie and Tim move out of sight to the other side of Kimberly's house.

"Ooooh," they say. "Who?"

"I don't know," I say. "A secret admirer."

Mama raises up on her elbows, lets the washrag fall from her eyes to her greased-up breasts. The look on her face causes my heartbeat to quicken, and I don't know whether to go on or to make up something juicy that'll make her happy.

"Let me guess," she says. She has studied my yearbooks, knows all the cute boys at school. "Jonathan Rivers?"

I shake my head, no.

"Ben Clonch?"

Nu-uh.

"Well, let's see it," she says, excitedly. "Hand it over, baby."

I pull the note from my library book where I've been saving it for her. I don't know if my heart is racing from the heatstroke I'm having or if it's because of the glorious smile on Mama's face. She unfolds the letter and squints against the white glare of the notebook paper. She squints harder and harder until her eyebrows stand down and her lips ease into a worrisome bunch.

"This is a girl's handwriting," she says.

"What?" I snatch the page to have another look. "No, it's *not.*"

"Look at all them curlicues," Mama says.

I study the writer's handwriting for clues, and she's right, the script is loopy and very well practiced. The letters are prim, and I wonder what that says about the writer's personality. Could the note actually be from *a girl?* I'm more baffled than before, when I thought a boy might like me.

"Stay away from them lizzies," Mama says sternly.

"Maybe it's just a joke," I offer, to make her feel better.

"A sick joke," she says.

"Maybe it's just a prissy boy who writes like a girl."

"Prissy boys are worse than lizzies. Stay away from the lot of them. Your daddy would have a fit if you brought home some little fairy-tailed boyfriend."

I am sorry I brought up the letter at all. I wipe sweat from my face with Mama's washrag, consider saying, "Well, what about a grown man named Tam? That's pretty queer sounding."

But she would just cock that sassy attitude, wink and smile, and say, "Oh, I beg to differ about that man, little girl," not saying what she's saying loud and clear. "And besides, that's different. You're young. Your whole life is in front of you."

Then in Tam's defense she would say, "There's just something about him," which is what she always says about men I'm "too young" to appreciate. "Trust your mama," she is always saying.

And I do. Most of the time. But I know this "trial separation" is just code for something more permanent. I've seen her lying in bed for days too often lately, and at times like that, I'm glad for Talmadge, glad as I can be. He's a nice man and gives Mama anything she wants, takes her out to eat. Invites me, too, often as not, though I never go. Tam is alright, I figure then.

I run my eyes over each character of my secret admirer's curvy handwriting.

"Maybe the letter is from someone trying to cheer me up," I offer again.

"Cheer you up about what?" Mama says.

* * *

It rains the next two weekends, so Kimberly and I are trapped inside playing jacks. I usually take all three throws before I toss a spread I can manage, but Kimberly has shown me how to work with whatever cluster of little metal stars that comes my way.

To practice, she makes me pick the jacks out of her hand. If she feels anything, even the slightest touch, I have to start over. We play in the kitchen where her mom has been trying all summer to root a houseplant in a glass of water. "Mother," Kimberly calls her. She is the only kid I know who calls her mom *Mother* that way.

In her room we lie on her bed and look at magazines with foldout posters of Erik Estrada and John Schneider.

We measure our chests with the measuring tape from her mother's sewing kit. We prime the roller balls of our lip gloss with our fingers and then smear gobs of sweet-smelling, chemical-tasting gloss over our lips. We want desperately to kiss someone.

Outside it's gray. Steam rises from our sidewalks, our driveways, even from the grass. Mama's tan is fading. "Rain is so depressing," she says. But I like it; I like the air before it rains, swirly and damp. I never really tan anyway. I am still peeling long runs of skin off my shins. Kimberly scratches at the pieces I can't reach on my back with her neat fingernails. I bite my nails, so I have to use the sharp point of a jack rock to bring up edges of dead skin that I can grab hold of.

"My uncle saw a man skinned alive in Vietnam," Kimberly says.

"Which one?" I ask.

"Tim," she says, and my heart hammers behind my training bra. "But they couldn't brainwash him," she says. "They never could."

* * *

I am flicking a big black bug off my blanket the following weekend—and picking away grass and little gnats that have stuck to my sweaty legs—when TJ Frazier strolls up to us in the yard. I grab my towel, standing, wrapping it around me, pretending I was just on my way inside. TJ is a boy in the neighborhood, a couple years older than me, a dropout whose eyes are permanently glassy from smoking pot all the time. He is cute, though, and I've always had a crush on him, so I don't know what to do when he stops and says, "Hello, foxy mamas."

Mama and Aunt Jonie fawn all over him; they could just eat him up, you can tell, even if he is just a kid. Precisely because he is just a kid.

He makes himself at home, flops down in my empty lawn chair beside Mama and says, "Want me to rub lotion on your beautiful body, Mrs. Lambert?"

I snatch the bottle of baby oil from him. "Grow up," I say.

He laughs and Mama and Aunt Jonie grin in cahoots with him.

"*All* of you," I say.

TJ reaches for my oatmeal cakes, unwraps one.

"Tabby has a secret admirer," Mama tells him.

"Mama! God!"

She looks at TJ with her spell-casting eyes and says, "Wasn't you, was it?"

He shoves the whole cake in his mouth, smiling dreamily, and I throw a book in front of my face and curse the day I was born. I am standing there with a big Marvin the Martian towel wrapped around my body, my legs and arms prickling from the smoldering look I know TJ is giving me. And he says, "The world is supposed to end in 2012."

I screw up my face behind the book, which is, I realize, what he's referring to.

Then he stretches out on my chair and stares up into the wild blue yonder as if he can see the end coming.

Mama and Aunt Jonie leer like headhunters.

TJ rolls over on one side, pulls his legs up in the fetal position, hands under one cheek and says, "But yeah, Tab. It was me."

He doesn't even go to my school, but my heart pounds to the song on the radio, "Tragedy" by the Bee Gees. I look like a complete retard standing there, so I drop my hands and make an attempt to glare at TJ, muster my surliest pose, as if to say, "In. Your. Dreams."

He sits up on one side of the foldout chair next to Mama with his hands hanging between his knees, looking at me with that stoned smile of his, those lazy eyes that bat in slow motion, and that distant-looking wry expression on his face.

Aunt Jonie starts gyrating in her chair to the Bee Gees and it is X-rated almost the way she writhes and thrusts her bony hips. TJ laughs, says, "Show me what you got, hot stuff," and sings along to the song. "Tragedy, when you lose control and you got no soul, it's tragedy." His voice is too low to stay with the Bee Gees, but he doesn't care. He stands up, struts, tears his T-shirt over his head, strikes a pose like something out of *Saturday Night Fever.*

His chest is scrawny and white, and he looks more like Mick Jagger, I think. He prances and sings and it is Mick Jagger exactly, nowhere near Barry Gibb, who is, we all agree, the cutest of the Bee Gees.

"That's horrible," I say, wanting to laugh, but wanting not to more. Aunt Jonie stands and dances with him; she is doing her "Lay Down, Sally" bit that drives me crazy it's so funny to watch, thrusting her pelvis and doing that "thumbing a ride" thing. Mama is going right along, singing and hooting at the two of them.

I seem to be the only one wondering if Donnie and Tim are getting an eye full across the way at Kimberly's house, and then there is Donnie, staring back with his mirrored sunglasses, reflecting a blinding ray of light that makes my eyes tear.

TJ and Aunt Jonie are boogieing around the backyard, shaking their tail feathers, doing what they know of the hustle. Part of me wants to show them some moves that are out of this world. But another part holds back. The sun is blistering hot now, and I feel like I might burst into flames. I read an article about a kid who spontaneously combusted when he had his first wet dream. TJ is stumbling and falling against Aunt Jonie, his hands like golden stars whizzing through the air.

Across the way, Tim is pushing the mower around the

playhouse where Kimberly and I used to play schoolteacher. He's taken off his shirt and turned his ball cap around backward.

Mama tells me, "Come on, Tab. *Live* a little." She's turning over, untying the strings of her bikini top so she won't get tan lines.

I think of leaving, slipping back inside the house, letting the door slam as I go, sure that no one would even miss me. Then I think of what I'll tell Mama later, when TJ is gone. I'll tell her he is a total pothead, and Aunt Jonie will say, "Yeah. But a cute pothead." As if that settles it.

* * *

When school is out and the sun is directly above the earth, scorching the Northern Hemisphere, Kimberly invites me to go swimming at a park that has water slides and go-karts. I take the money Daddy has given me for my birthday to buy a new striped beach towel, something mature and inconspicuous, and a bathing-suit cover-up to hide my fat hips. I don't know how to swim, but Kimberly says she can teach me. She doesn't mention that her uncles are coming or that I will have to sit between them in the backseat of her mother's Mazda, which barely has room for Kimberly and me. I think of asking if I can ride in the front seat, but I don't want to seem ungrateful. Kimberly gets carsick riding in the back.

Mama would have a cow if she knew the uncles are coming, not because she'd object but because she'd be jealous and think it a waste of a good opportunity for another woman, an older woman like herself. What can I do? I'm just a kid. I hope she doesn't see us piling into Kimberly's mother's car.

Donnie is wearing a pair of short white trunks with a yellow-and-blue stripe around the middle and a belly shirt that shows the lower half of his hairy stomach. Tim is wearing plaid knee-length trunks and a baggy T-shirt with Mickey Mouse on it, silent Mickey from the old black-and-white cartoons.

I wait until given instructions about where to sit, but eventually I must climb between the men in the backseat who sprawl out with their legs thrown wide open like a couple of Venus flytraps, and I try my best not to touch them. They are hairy everywhere, and my bare thighs prickle with the feel of their legs touching mine. I wrap my towel over my lap and make myself as small as possible. I think of Mama's spell-casting eyes and the hold they had on TJ Frazier, a boy not even half her age, and feel a surge of power inside me like a burning tornado, a volcano turned inside out. My arms and feet look brown inside the car. My white toenails gleam in the floorboard straddling the hump between Donnie's sandaled feet and Tim's sockless Converse sneakers.

Donnie throws his arm up over the seat behind me, clearly cramped, and asks if I'd be more comfortable sitting on his lap. The heat inside the car is a greenhouse trapping the sun. I smell the sweat of Donnie's armpit and feel myself melting into the vinyl seat beneath me, the sweat of my own legs and the sweat of two grown men running together and pooling in the seat of my swimsuit.

"No thanks," I shoot back too quickly, feeling the heat rise in my face.

"You guys okay back there?" Kimberly's mother asks, glancing into the rearview.

Donnie pumps the window down and reaches across me to the other window on Tim's side of the car.

"I got it," Tim says. "Watch it!" Heavy beads of sweat have collected in the short hair follicles around his face, and when he leans forward to roll down the window, I see that the back of his

T-shirt is beginning to soak through. His shirt is bunched up over his trunks, and I see a dark line of matted hair disappearing into the small of his back.

Kimberly's mother fires up the Mazda and soon the wind rushes through the open windows, wicking away sweat from the surface of our skin.

"Goddamn if it's not hot," Donnie says.

Without a word, Tim cuts his eyes at his brother and glowers, and Donnie says, "*What?*"

The melting lard of my fat thighs pressing against him is irritating Donnie, but I dare not lean closer to Tim or my skin will burn to a crisp. I perch as best I can on the hump between my legs and lean forward between the seats where I don't have to look at the men.

Kimberly smiles and leans to whisper something in my ear. She turns my jaw toward Tim, pushes my hair behind my ear, and cups her hands to the side of my head. I blush from the nearness of Tim's face to mine, notice the little whiskers of missed hairs under his lip, and he smiles without showing his teeth. I smile, too, feel a cyclone of bees in my heart, and think that I can almost taste the smell of Kimberly's Bubblicious bubble gum. There is a dead wasp in the window behind us, a little rubber smiley face on the tip of the car's antenna rising behind it. My bare back is exposed and I feel Kimberly's hands cupping my ear, her pink breath forming one word after another. "My uncle told me you were pretty."

"Which one?" I ask, the words collapsing in my throat.

Tim's green eyes crinkle at the edges when he smiles at me.

"Show Uncle Tim your mood ring, Tabby," Kimberly says.

I lift my hand and lower my eyes, grinning, and he circles his palm around two of my fingers to get a better look. "Purple," he says. "What mood is that?"

Kimberly giggles and pushes my shoulder.

"You try it," I say, sliding the ring off my hand and holding it up between two digits.

He offers his pinky to me and I blush. "You have to wait for the color to drain," I say, waving the ring in the air. "Okay, now."

He extends his pinky again and I cup his wrist in the palm of my left hand, the tips of his curled fingers like live wires sending sparks up my arm. I wedge the band over the knuckle of his finger, and it stops midway. "Too tight?" I ask. He shakes his head, smiles again, and we wait for the ring to perform its magic.

Kimberly's other uncle, Donnie, fidgets in the seat beside me. He picks up his legs and I feel my skin separating from his, a cool rush of air rolling between us.

"Blue," Tim says after a minute or so, turning the ring so we can see it. "Is that good?"

Kimberly punches my shoulder. "Yes!" she says, nudging harder.

I shake my head. "It's just because we're all sweaty," I say, thinking to myself that I will never take this ring off my finger *ever* again now that he has touched it. My skin flushes hotter and I reach across Donnie's side of the car for cooler air out the window. Tim tries to pull the ring off his finger, but it doesn't budge.

My hair lashes into Donnie's face, and he grabs me by the waist. I'm startled and latch onto Kimberly's seat in front of me. Tim yanks at the ring. Donnie's big thumbs press hard into the small of my back. Then he tugs once, twice, and I am up onto his hot, sticky lap.

The wind from the window whips in my face, steals my breath, and I think I will smother. The pitch of Donnie's knee drives my head into the liner of the car's ceiling and I wrestle as he tries to pull me into a more comfortable position against his stomach. I arch my back, crane my neck, and all I can see are Tim's calloused hands, my mood ring still biting into the flesh of his pinky. He throws his palms up in urgency, signaling for Donnie to stop.

"What?" Donnie says. *"She's only fourteen years old,"* and the mention of my age in Tim's presence sends hot gasses to my eyes. I don't know how old he is, but it's a lot older than fourteen. I don't have so much as a pair of sunglasses to protect myself, so when the tears come I bury my face in the stupid new towel I bought with the birthday money from my father.

Tim brings his pinky up to his mouth and my mood ring disappears inside as he wets his finger and tries again to twist it free from his hand. He yanks and the ring lets go. He hands it to me, and I scramble out of Donnie's lap back to the hump.

"Everything okay back there?" Kimberly's mother tries to get a look at what's happening.

I press myself between the bucket seats in front of me, crying, and slide the ring back onto my finger. "Honey, are you okay?" she asks. "What happened?"

"Nothing," I say.

Behind me, I hear Tim cluck his tongue at Donnie, and it is the sound of a star swallowing its own planet.

* * *

I call Mama from a pay phone as soon as we arrive at the pool. Pretend to be sick. Wet kids with towels draped over their shoulders beg for Pop Rocks and banana Popsicles.

"What is it?" Mama asks. "George?" George is code for that time of the month. It's not George, but I lie and say that it is so she will come right away and get me. She would never want me to be trapped in a bathing suit in public with George.

I wait in the glassed-in arcade, the sounds of pinballs and asteroids circling me as I watch Kimberly's uncles teaching her how to dive backward from the springboard. Donnie does backflips and cannonballs, bounding down the length of the board in thunderous lunges. When he emerges, he crosses his hairy brown shoulders in front of himself on the edge of the pool and rests, flashing a smile at the young mothers dipping their babies in the kiddie pool across the way.

Tim walks to the end of the board, aligns his body with his arms extended above his head. Standing perfectly still until he is ready to leap. He does graceful swan dives and snappy jackknives, his long body folding and unfolding in the sun. He slices through the water without a ripple, swimming the whole length of the pool underwater, his body a shimmering comet tearing through space and time.

I hold out my hand, gaze upon my ring, its colors swirling.

Black Shuck

At first it had only been rabies that concerned him. The dog had come around once or twice, and after watching it from a distance, Stephen hadn't seen it swagger at all the way the raccoon in the news clips had. Every day or so, one TV station or another was flashing the map again, showing the spread of rabies across the state over the past ten years. Forsyth County had been one of the last, but now a farmer had reported a diseased cow. A cow, of all creatures. The sound bite alone had nearly given Stephen nightmares, prompting him to pay heed. He'd stopped throwing scraps out along the edge of the woods for whatever animal that came upon them. Before, it had seemed like the charitable thing to do, but now he was wary of drawing scavengers. He'd noticed the stray right off, but because it was a black Lab like his childhood dog, he waited before calling animal control. Not that he was crazy about calling them anyway. You didn't have to be a dog lover to know the result of that.

This one wasn't a full-blooded Labrador. It had a slightly longer muzzle like maybe it had some German shepherd in it, and it was a bit bigger than a Lab. As a child he'd grown up with his older brother's Lab, and although Bingo had been essentially the family pet, Stephen had never had a dog of his own. And now this one had come to him, chosen him, it seemed. He imagined the stray, marveling alongside him, tilting its head curiously at the squawking clouds of approaching birds that more frequently seemed to settle by the hundreds into one giant pin oak on his property, a tree that readily absorbed them like so many molecules of carbon dioxide. Strange to see so many birds at once, and so often coming to the same tree. But it was strange days, he was reminded.

Misfit, he'd taken to calling the stray. "Turn up at a time like this," he said, rubbing its thick neck, "bound to be trouble." But secretly he harbored a boyish hope. What genuine joy did he have in his life of late? Katie had become brittle and, he hated to admit it, superficial as well. Nothing had the look of reality to it anymore. Not her, not the house. He was smothering under all the fake happiness, the kiss-ass, corporate phoniness that had body-snatched her from him years ago. He was lonely, he admitted to himself. He needed something real, even if trouble might be attached.

He thought of his English granddad, fearful of strays, particularly ones with dark coats. "Black shuck," he called them, a portent of bad times.

But as far as Stephen was concerned, bad times were what he'd been living. Life was supposed to be messy. That's what he and Katie'd forgotten over the years, trying so hard to keep things looking happy.

Anyway, there were lots of old wives' tales. Some contradictory, that a black dog was a harbinger of good things, a protector.

It was hard not to be a little superstitious, though. A black shuck often turned up before drownings and house fires, his grandfather said. They foretold nervous collapses and death.

But the resemblance of Misfit to Bingo had him squarely on the fence. The dog had barely bowed its back when Stephen bent to the ground and pretended to pick up rocks. "Get!" he'd said, but the stray had wagged its whole body and edged closer until Stephen had finally brought home a bag of kibbles. It was just a bony old dog. What harm could it do?

* * *

A couple weeks later, Stephen noticed a truck slowing as it passed his house. An old man was driving, and he hunched over the steering wheel to bend and look up into Stephen's yard. He made several passes, turning around in neighbors' driveways before he finally pulled up alongside Stephen's mailbox and called out his passenger-side window. "Hear you got a stray come around," he said.

Stephen nodded. Even though the vet had told him the stray had heartworms that would require an expensive surgery, he had grown fond of the idea of keeping the dog. No rabies, at least. "Missing one?" Stephen asked the old timer.

"Just a stray to me, too, but I've had him near a year now," the old man said. "Get to pining for one after that long."

Stephen smiled, then leaning casually into the window of the truck, a rusted-out Toyota, looked inside at the heap of mail spilling over the seat and across a Bible in a worn leather cover. The Bible had fallen between the plastic cup-console in the floorboard. He was compelled to push the mail away from the book, out of family custom. His mother had thought it a sacrilege to put anything on top of a Bible, though Stephen surmised that maybe this one had gotten more use than even theirs had. Stephen hadn't been to church in his adult life though, so he didn't suppose it mattered how the old man handled his own Bible.

Stephen looked around the rest of the truck cab. Several dead flies had gotten wedged between the window and the dash. He imagined their wings crumbling into ashes at the slightest touch. There were no floor mats, and as Stephen noted this he saw, too, that the old man wore no socks and that his pants had come unhemmed.

"He a brown dog?" the old man asked.

"Black," Stephen said.

"Brownish-black. Kindly big like one of them lifesaving kind?"

"Pretty attached to him, are you?"

"Ain't no good for nothing, really, just lays round most time. But I guess I've got kind of fond of him." The old man looked over Stephen's shoulder up into the yard. "Care if I see wuther he's mine or not?"

"Go ahead," said Stephen. He didn't mind turning the animal over to its owner. What need did he have for it? "Pull into the driveway and come on around back. I'm keeping him chained so animal control doesn't catch him. Lot of rabies this year. Probably heard."

"Nope. But old Blue ain't got the rabies."

"Name's Blue?"

"I'as trying to be different." The old man cut a pulpy-looking smile at Stephen. "Pull up there, you say?"

Stephen nodded and backed away from the vehicle to let it pass. When the old man had parked, Stephen opened his door and led him through a yard plagued by drought and crabgrass around behind the house.

The dog was chained to a stake Stephen had driven into the ground, and upon the men's arrival, the dog lay in the same spot without even lifting its head.

"Look here, Blue," the man said, but the dog didn't respond. "Blue's been a heap of help to me at the chicken houses."

"That so?"

"Oh, yeah. I been working them damned old houses for years, and now I got the chance to owner-finance them from the man I been working for."

Stephen nodded. "That's great. And what's Blue do down at the farm?"

"Just lays around, naturally. He's a dog. But he's a lucky bastard, and I got to get him back," the old man said. He squinted for a better look, and for a second, Stephen thought he didn't recognize the animal.

"That him? That your Blue?" he asked, pointing to a spot in the yard under a stand of pine trees where grass had again been beaten out, this time by moss. After the recent rains, the moss was soft again and clean for the dog to lie upon.

"Oh yeah," the man said, stopping to look and to rest. "That's him alright. I'd know that dog anywhere."

"He's not too lucky, though," Stephen said. "He's sick."

"Yep, he takes spells." The old man resumed hobbling toward the dog.

"Vet says he's eaten up with heartworms," Stephen said then. "I had him looked at."

"That so?" The man paused for a second as if he might be considering the loss of Blue for good. Then he said, "The days of all creatures, large or small, is marked anyhow. He's got a lot of age on him, in dog years you know, like me."

When he reached the tree line, the old man started to kneel beside the dog but hesitated and stood back.

"You sure this is him?" Stephen said. "He's real sick and needs treatment." He was beginning to worry about turning the dog over to the old man.

"Dogs know how to take care of their selves. He'll get out and find some grass to chew. They just eat certain ones for certain ailments. None here to be had," he said, grinning amiably at Stephen, who smiled wanly in return.

"I'm willing to keep the dog and pay for the treatment," Stephen said, redirecting the man's attention to the stray, which was panting hard now for no apparent reason on an early autumn day. "I think your dog might *look* like this one but be older. This one's less than a year old."

"Well, that can't be," said the old man. "I've had him now near a year and he was full-growed when he come to me."

Stephen guessed then that if the dog really was the old man's, all his misgivings about the dog being a black shuck were just nonsense. The old man had had the dog a year, he said, and he hadn't fallen victim to any catastrophes. In fact, the old man believed the dog had brought him good luck.

"What did you say your name was again?" Stephen asked.

"Garl McEvoy," the man said, staring down at the dog and clicking his tongue. "Look here, Blue." The dog stretched in the sun and unfurled its tongue in a long, slow yawn, but didn't lift its head.

"That's what I'm saying. Your dog must look like this one."

"It is this one, mister. I know my own damn dog."

The tone of the old man's voice took on a sharpness that gave Stephen a moment's hesitation. Suppose he whipped out a gun and pointed it at him?

"Why don't you take your big money and buy your own dog?"

"I didn't mean to offend you. I don't even want a dog," Stephen said. "My wife—. It's just that—"

"If you don't want him, then what's the matter?"

"I just want to make sure he's looked after."

"You some kind of good Samaritan or something? I know how to look after my own dog. Come on, Blue." The old man unhooked the dog's collar and led it by the nape of the neck to his truck.

* * *

That evening, Stephen pulled out the pamphlet the vet had given him and read again about the dangers of heartworms. He remembered the Doberman's heart in the specimen jar, how it had looked stuffed with spaghetti. "I'm never eating spaghetti again," he told Katie. "Don't ever fix it."

"Fine. Don't worry."

"It looked like a big mushroom full of spaghetti," he added.

"Alright already. No more spaghetti; I got it."

Stephen thought then about the mushrooms along the edge of the woods where he'd taken Misfit to relieve himself. They'd grown right up out of the dog's rain-soaked turds, but he'd also seen them deep in the woods. All kinds. More damn mushrooms than he'd ever seen in his life. It was some kind of crazy year for them. They came in all sorts of colors and sizes. Some were round and white as golf balls and others were a foot tall, flat as plates. He had the sudden urge to check the *Farmers' Almanac*, which he'd never before consulted, though he'd always been attracted by its mystical reputation for predicting crop conditions and weather as far as a year out.

When he and Katie were in college, some guy at a party had passed around a jug of what he claimed was a certain kind of mushroom juice that induced near-death experiences. Stephen had been strictly a weed man back then and hadn't imbibed, but Katie had. She'd fallen to the floor like a sack of flour without making so much as a whimper, but Stephen had thought it was all a hoax. She was needy like that then. She'd had a miscarriage that year and seemed to crave the sympathy it evoked. Stephen had been too immature to be anything but grateful at the time—he had no intentions of marrying Katie or anyone else. It wasn't until he'd blown the LSATs that he resigned to marriage and then they discovered they couldn't have kids, which was ironic because then—now—he wanted them more than anything. Katie claimed to have seen her life flash before her eyes. "I saw it," she'd said, "my baby," which sounded to Stephen like she'd been fishing for pity.

Funny he remembered that now. He wondered if all these weird things, the long drought, the rampant cases of rabies, the mushrooming population of mushrooms, had something to do with the end times he'd grown up hearing about. Two women had knocked on his door recently and handed him a booklet on biological terrorism and what the Bible has to say about it. Somehow, though, none of that stuff about al-Qaeda or North Korea worried him like knowing that somewhere out there was a sad-sack dog with heartworms. And maybe a black shuck, at that. Or maybe a protector in these troubling times. The old man thought so, at least. Dogs were like children— someone had to look out for their interests. He thought again of the Doberman's heart, exploding with parasites that belonged on the ends of fishing lines.

He remembered, as a boy, digging night crawlers in the woods, under the rotting leaves and felled trees. It occurred to him now how energy transfers itself from one form to another. Tree bark turns right back into dirt. A pile of shit begets a mushroom, which lands in somebody's plate of spaghetti. Reincarnation, he thought. Reincarnation. The black shuck; he had to save it or something bad was going to happen.

* * *

He knew Katie would think it was crazy. "You want to what?" she would say. "Find him and offer to pay for the surgery anyway? *Honey*." And he didn't dare try and make her understand the transference of energy. "Reincarnation, Stephen? What are you saying?"

Instead, he waited till daylight and then got up and found the old man's number in the phone book. Garl McEvoy, he remembered. It was early, yeah, but the old timers get up before sunrise, he knew. Garl had chickens to tend.

"Listen," he said when he had the man on the line. "I'd like to pay for Misfit, er, Blue's heartworm treatment. His appointment is the twenty-sixth at 9 a.m. You just drop him off—or I can even come by and take him for you."

"I don't want your damn charity," the old man said, perhaps annoyed by his keen memory of meeting Stephen.

"We got off on the wrong foot, but I'm really not an asshole or anything. I'm just worried about the dog."

"I think you're crazy is what I think."

Stephen sighed. "I only want to help."

"Well, you're too late anyway. The dogcatcher come and took him. I think. Or else he's wandered off again. No telling. But listen. I've got to get that dog back. The inspectors are trying to shut down my houses. Double-laying houses won't pass regulations no more. I got to have that dog."

So it was true, Stephen thought. The black shuck was bringing doom just as his grandfather had warned. He called the pound, but the receptionist said they hadn't come across a dog registered to a Stephen Philips. "You sure?" he asked. "He may have lost his tags."

"We do have a chocolate Lab-mix," she said then. "Male, but without proof of ownership, you'd have to adopt him."

"Brown or black?" he asked.

"Brown."

"Hold onto him," Stephen said. "I'll be right there."

* * *

On the way to the pound, he stopped and pawned his toolbox and every piece of Craftsman he owned to cover the seventy-five dollar adoption fee. He'd used the tools about as often as Katie fired up one of the many appliances she owned. He could've pawned the bread machine and she'd never know.

When he got there, the dog was barking and jumping up against the kennel, which made Stephen wonder if this was the same animal. Then he noticed the dog had a white spot on its chest. "It's not him," he told the animal control officer. "Mine's part German shepherd."

"Uh-huh," the officer said. "This the only Lab-mix we got." He looked at a chart on a clipboard. "Brought in last Friday."

The dog barked and wagged its tail like a pup, though it looked a few years old to Stephen. He wondered if maybe the dog was Garl's. "Here, Blue," he called, and the dog jumped and barked again, though he knew it was no sign he recognized the name. "Came in Friday, you say?"

The officer bobbed his head.

The dog's time was almost up. Stephen knew it. He could spring it and take it home to Garl, but why should he? The old bastard probably wouldn't give his money back. And then Misfit might turn up and he'd be short what he needed for the heartworms.

He knelt in front of the cage and a sudden whiff of stinking wet dog hit him in the face. He looked down the row. Dogs of every size and breed jumped against the chain-link fencing or pawed at the concrete slab that ran the length of the building. The barking was riotous and Stephen noticed that he hadn't heard them when he'd entered through the front.

"You decided?" the officer asked, and Stephen turned to face him. How could a guy work in such a place?

"I bet you've got quite a few at home yourself," Stephen said.

"Just one."

"Get him here?"

"Nah. It's the wife's."

Stephen nodded, scratched his head. "I'll tell you. I just can't choose," he said.

"Alright."

"Saving one's better than nothing though."

The officer bobbed his head. "Yeah."

"You all should just give them away. If people want them, I mean," Stephen said.

"That's why they're here, cause of people who wanted them. We have to make sure they're fixed, get their shots. People won't take it upon themselves. If a person can't afford that, they can't feed one either."

Stephen looked down the row at the pugs and pekineses, the chows and hounds and terriers, at the certifiable mutts with faces innocent as babies.

He turned to the officer. "I'll take him."

* * *

But by the time Stephen had a chance to deliver Blue to old Garl McEvoy's house, the guy had blown his head off with a shotgun. His two broke-ass sons who lived in the shitty little trailer with him said Garl had come home distraught, that the inspectors had shut down his chicken houses and old Garl didn't know how he was supposed to make the mortgage now. His former boss had screwed him over, as he'd been aware of the new regulations when he'd owner-financed the double-laying houses to Garl.

"My God," said Stephen. "I'm sorry for your loss."

"Daddy reached into the fridge for a beer, but we'd already drunk the last one," said one of the sons. "Then he just hauled ass to the back of the trailer and blowed his brains out."

Stephen could hardly believe what he was hearing. But then it got worse for old Garl. His sons said they couldn't afford a funeral, so they'd donated his body to the whole body donation program at the teaching hospital in Winston. He'd just been picked up the day before.

What the hell, Stephen thought to himself. Black shuck. Everything his grandfather said was true.

* * *

"You're being ridiculous," Katie said when he explained what had happened to Garl and why Stephen thought it was the black shuck that had brought it upon him.

"If I don't find that dog and have it looked after by a vet, Katie," he said, "something real bad is going to happen to us."

"Baby," Katie said. "Listen to what you're saying. That's old hillbilly superstition. Stop it, okay? Just forget the stupid dog already."

But Stephen couldn't forget it. And he couldn't find it either. Misfit had up and disappeared. Stephen plastered the neighborhood with missing dog posters, went door to door, knocking. He followed leads going nowhere, searched local animal shelters' websites. Weeks and weeks turned into months, then a year and more weeks. Stories of rabies slowly faded away, only to be replaced by something else. Meningitis was on the rise again, strangely, after decades of being managed. Avian bird flu after that. Lead paint. Swine flu. Trans fats, SARS, MRSA, anthrax.

Stephen scoured the news expectantly, dreadful, but nothing turned up on his own doorstep. Not even misfortune. But it was coming. One day soon it would be there.

Rasputin's Remarkable Sleight of Hand

Every night Rasputin chose a different one to come forward and go inside the box of blades. Always they were pretty, and always they were thin, T-tiny thin like snakes, wearing green eye shadow and T-shirts revealing trim young abdomens. People thought it was a hoax: all the girls were plants. Rasputin was insulted.

Or so it would seem.

Each summer a certain number of locals appeared in the stands, spewing their skepticism, some claiming to know him. "Ain't you kin?" one or two might say. Or, "Ain't you that little youngin' from Tally Town?" "Ain't you that Greek?" "Ain't you that Mexican?" "That Russian?" "That Indian?" "Didn't we go to school together?" "Ain't we worked together somewheres?"

His response like that of a giant puppet: he'd throw up his arms until they snapped at the elbow, bend mechanically at the waist, and slap his knee, allowing his great jaw to fall open in a stagey guffaw. "Do I amooze you?" he'd say, laughing, as he held his make-believe belly. "Ha! Ha! Ha!"

"That ain't your real name," someone would yell, then turn to his neighbor. "That ain't even his real his name," this fella would insist, folks nodding in agreement, others shaking no-they-didn't-knows.

Rasputin would humor them, let them cajole. This was the show, after all. This was what they came for summer upon summer. Out from the little hollows where they clambered bent-backed into the earth to mine the black diamonds that enslaved them. Poor creatures. How quickly they tired of the tilt-a-whirl, the house of mirrors. But his . . . his was an act of notoriety, the carnival owners turning a handsome profit from Rasputin's renowned sleight of hand.

People were inclined to believe in magic. It was what they wanted, never mind what they said. Magician. Preacher. Politician. They all dealt in the art of misdirection. Look at this hand while I pull a rabbit out of this sleeve over here. Nothing that couldn't be spotted by the naked eye, of course, one that cared to look. Though none did.

"I am known by many names!" he would exclaim with a delicate fingering of his handsomely oiled mustache. "Ask about me in Buchanan County, and folks there will tell you I'm Agamemnon. Them in Logan and Mingo call me Zorba, the Greek! Oh, yes! I know your little hamlets well, for I, too, have toiled in the great black belly of these earthen hills."

Just then a deeply tanned blond wearing a long plumage of feathers in her cap would appear on stage, pushing a cart upon which lay a large item concealed by a scarlet-colored pashmina with long fringes. Momentarily, all would fall silent and stare as Rasputin made his way to the center of the stage and asked for a volunteer from the audience.

"Anyone?" he would ask, theatrically peering out, scout-style, hand held over his deep-set eyes, entertainingly gazing out upon the sea of arms waving in the little aluminum stands.

"Is there no one at all?" he would tease, as some took to standing and hollering, stamping their brogans against the steel girders.

He would rip the pashmina away quite handily as the crowd leaned forward, squinting to have a better look at what lay beneath. "I will need the assistance of an expert. Any geologists in the audience?" Hands would fall, slowly at first, as each person turned neighbor to neighbor to inquire, "A what?"

"Any coal miners then?" Up they would shoot again!

"You there," he would say, pointing. "You sir, yes." Then he would whisper to the overly tanned blond, who would usher the man down through the stands and up two, three, four steps and onto the rickety little stage. The man would turn and smile at the audience, throw up a hand maybe at someone he might recognize.

"Sir, if you will kindly identify for our audience what this object before you is. Have you any notion at all?"

The man would laugh. "Why yeah," he would say. "That's a big chunk of coal."

"Thank you," Rasputin would say cheerily. "And will you examine it more closely?"

Now the man would bend nearer and study upon it with all seriousness. His reputation was at stake, after all. "Bituminous," he would add, proudly.

"Yes, I can see you know your geology, sir." Rasputin would ask for a round of applause. "Now tell us if you care to, sir, in your expert opinion, what are those markings located just there and there on the chunk of coal before you?"

The man would reach a hand forward to rub his fingers in the grooves, smoothly etched in the form of a fern. "I can't rightly say. Looks like a flower of some kind. A plant. The branch of a tree maybe."

"And how old would you estimate that this chunk of coal is, sir? Can you venture a guess?"

"A thousand years old or better, I suppose. Couldn't be no more than that, though, if what the Bible says is true."

"But a thousand years old, at least, would you say?"

"Yes, it come from the earth. It's a rock."

"A thousand years," Rasputin would repeat. "Well before our time then? Is that fair to say?"

"Oh, yes. It's way older'n us."

The tanned blond would glide across the stage again, this time carrying a little pickaxe.

"Would you be so kind as to strike this piece of coal with this implement, sir? I'm sure you know how to handle one of these."

The miner would then roll up his sleeves, exposing his flinty little arms. "Happy to," he'd say before bringing the axe down sharply and splintering the lump of coal into several smaller pieces.

Rasputin would then step forward and poke around in the coal shards until, "Yes!" he would exclaim. "Would you take a look at this?" Then he would bring up a Timex watch, slightly sullied but still ticking. He would hand it over to the man for examination.

"How in the devil did that get in there?" the man would question. He'd press it to his ear. "Still running!" Then he'd turn to the crowd and hold it up in disbelief.

But as with any act, the "ticking Timex in the lump of coal" trick had lost its razzle-dazzle after a few summers. Now the natives were restless again. There were cell phones to compete with nowadays, after all. People snapping selfies with Rasputin in the background to post on Facebook but otherwise having very little actual interest in his truly remarkable sleight of hand.

One night, to prove his greatness, he filled the tent with sulfur and, using mentalism, chose a different girl. No more skinnies. This time he chose a fat girl. Fat, fat. So fat no one could harp and complain anymore. Just as easily, he could have read her lips as her mind, for she mouthed along to his every magic word. *Majook! Majook! Sarupy!* Her fleshy lips protruding. He spotted her there like a bale of hay on the farthest most bench, sitting utterly to herself, her mind fizzing with whimsy. He called her forward and gave her a wilting rose. She put on a stage frown. He waved a hand, restoring its bloom. She smiled. No one clapped.

Then, lying bare chested on a bed of broken glass, he had the fat girl stand upon his back. The crowd clapped, more or less, but it was not enough. They wanted the fat girl inside the box of blades. In she went.

Rasputin donned his cape, caressed together his delicate hands. When they had paid their dollar to walk across the stage and peer down inside the box, they would see there was no fooling; the blades were real, the girl was real and fat, and there was no room for the fat girl to twist around all those blades. And how was Rasputin going to pull that off?

"It is worth two dollars," Rasputin said. "You will not believe it; it is the greatest feat of all time."

He pulled six great sabers from red velvet sheaths and laid them across the brightly painted wooden box. Each one gleamed with spellbinding ghastliness. To demonstrate their razor sharpness, he slit the bellies of watermelons, filleted mutton with ease—cut venison, ham hocks, whole sides of beef.

The audience sat smirking. Watermelons. *Hmph.* "Big deal," they harried.

Rasputin flung back his satin-lined cape and shoved the first deadly blade into the box. The fat girl with yellow eyes cried, "Ooooww!"

Rasputin flinched and bent to her. "Alright, my darling?"

The crowd did not respond. They yawned.

"Sorry," she said.

Rasputin held the second blade overhead, then slowly, slowly, slowly pierced the box. He felt the pinch of the fat girl's flesh upon the saber, nearly heard a squeak as if perhaps she were made of cork. He paused. The crowd jeered, threw popcorn. Rasputin sunk the knife deeper, deeper, deeper until he felt the scrape of bone against blade. The fat girl shut her yellow eyes, grated her blunt teeth. The crowd bawled obscenities.

So it went each time, a slow and torturous tear through the corpulent body of the fat girl with yellow eyes. Her great round face paled with each mighty thrust of Rasputin's blade.

Finally, it was done. The crowd paid two dollars and walked across the stage to peer inside. There was the fat girl, brimming over the sides of the box, squared like so much dough pounded into a bread pan. They could not see the blades at all, only the blade handles outside the box. "Something's wrong," they said. "This is a trick box." They demanded to stand around close while Rasputin pulled out all the knives so they could see.

"Five dollars each," Rasputin said. They paid. It was worth every cent in their pockets to disprove Rasputin. And if they couldn't do it today, they would be back tomorrow, or the day after, or the one after that until the whole damn summer was over.

He pulled the blades out slowly, with all the dramatic flourish they were accustomed to. They waited patiently, more or less. "Alright, already," they said. Rasputin would not be hurried. He looked deeply into the yellow eyes of the fat girl who lay inside his box. She was transfixed by his mustache, by his shiny black eyes, he imagined. And she was. The fat girl with yellow eyes had been to every show and had grown fat there on the bleachers of Rasputin's Remarkable Sleight of Hand, eating funnel cakes and homemade fudge from the ladies' auxiliary.

Rasputin held her hand. The coming out would be worse than the going in, he explained. She knew it would. He tugged at the first blade; it snagged. The audience harrumped. "More tricks!" They narrowed their eyes, tapped their sneakers on the plywood stage. Rasputin yanked, and out it came, bloody red with an organ dangling from its tip. The fat girl's heart. The audience leaped back and gasped, then leaned forward. "Hot damn," they said.

Rasputin was bewildered. The heart beat wildly. The fat girl lay calmly inside. She looked peaceful, but glum. Docile. Her yellow eyes locked wet and sticky onto the black eyes of Rasputin. He trembled. The audience guffawed. They liked seeing Rasputin's cunning, his very acumen, laid bare in such a way. They did not know he was the real deal. Rasputin, himself, did not know it.

Only the fat girl with yellow eyes knew it.

Ever so gently, he plucked the girl's heart from the tip of his blade and carefully laid it inside his satin-lined hat, standing next to a wand and a crystal ball on a velvet-covered, claw-footed table. The heart was big, like the girl, enormous really. It squished down inside the hat but rose up its tall, tall sides and beat red and blue mists of blood droplets that spritzed up from the top of the hat with each great quivering pulse.

Pearls of perspiration popped out on Rasputin's bushy brows. The girl will die, he feared. I'll be chased by pitchfork. He hurried with the rest of the blades. Each came out like the first. Mired in the blood and bodily fluids of the fat girl with yellow eyes, a different organ swinging from the sharp point of every blade. The gory liver, the gray lungs, the waggling intestines. Rasputin didn't know where to put them all. He stuffed them in his pockets to keep them from being trampled on by the crowd.

The fat girl was speechless. Rasputin kneeled before the box and spoke to her. He stretched out beside her and wept. The crowd laughed. Rasputin had lost his marbles. They wanted to see something else, but he only lay there on the step beside the box. "Get up," they said, kicking his shiny patent leather shoes, tugging on his split-tailed coat. "What's this? You're just going to lay there? You suck, Rasputin. You were never all that good. We're out of here, and we *won't* be back tomorrow." They ditched the finale, peeved and bitching.

The fat girl tried to speak, but she was in awe of Rasputin. Her mouth was dry. "I love you" was all she could say, enough to rouse Rasputin to kiss her lips.

"Why?" he asked. "Why?"

"Because you're magical," she said.

But Rasputin didn't feel magical. He felt old. He *was* old. Very, very old, hundreds of years old. And this was what the fat girl loved most. She rolled her yellow eyes to look at Rasputin lying on the step beside her. He stared up at the ceiling, spoke of his long, long life, of all the great loves he had known, all the great losses, of victories, and addictions, and illnesses. She had never seen him up so close. Her yellow eyes fell over his face. It was not a perfect face. Some thought it odd looking, but the fat girl with yellow eyes found it beautiful, even at such close proximity, when every deep crag shone out from the corners of his shiny, black eyes. She loved every line, felt small enough to fall inside them and travel to all the places he had ever been through all the eons of his existence. She studied his ear because it was the feature most easy to see from her awkward vantage point inside the tight, little box.

It was a glorious ear. Two deep furrows of flesh lay hidden just between the ear and his long-handled sideburn, and she felt so thrilled at having had that special glimpse of him, a glimpse no one she knew would ever have, that she was satisfied in a deep and lasting way she knew she would never be again.

"I should go," she said.

"Go where?"

"Home," she said. He did not ask where she lived, and she imagined it was because he could not really conjure what such a thing was, home. She thought of him sleeping in rooming houses next door to girls of the night who probably he slept with, or else in trailers back behind fairground fences where the air was choked with the smell of elephant dung and cigarette smoke and the fumes of generators.

She sat upright in the box. "I wish you'd stay," he said. She wanted to. For a fleeting second, she dreamed of staying, of being part of his show somehow. But what would she do? She had no talent of any kind, no beauty, no wit or charm. She was just a fat girl from Bramwell with faintly yellow eyes.

He seemed desperate, though, afraid of something. He needed her company like no one had ever needed it before. He needed *her*. She was the only person in all the world whose company he wanted, craved, had to have. Any number of things might happen to her later, during the course of her own long life. She might marry; have children; slim down, maybe; become a Pilates instructor; take up sudoku. But nothing would bring her to the edge of herself this way again, the brink of her very soul, looking at another human being who was not really human at all but something else entirely, something ethereal, something beyond her flesh, his flesh, all flesh altogether, something she could only think of as breath. Hers, his. It was the same. And it flickered like a candle and was gone as quickly as she could think of it.

She imagined the two of them outside the red-curtained theatre, no funny hats or velvet vests. No props or disguises.

Just the two of them, walking the fairgrounds, watching kids sneak drags from stolen cigarettes; standing in line for slaw dogs just like anybody else, just like she herself did on any given summer night. But it was all a fantasy. He might turn into a pillar of salt.

So she leaned back into the box and stayed a while longer. But even as she did, she felt all of time sucking away at this spectacular moment. A million things ran through her mind, but they were distant and hazy. She cursed herself for being dense in every way; even her mind was fat, she thought. She wanted to remember everything; she batted her yellow eyes like flashbulbs. An ashtray, she thought. Had he just recently smoked a cigarette? He turned on his side still lying beside her on the step, and yes, she smelled the cigarette on his breath, and she had never loved a smell as much in her life. It was arid but not foul; it was the smell of thirst.

She wished he would levitate her, send her high into the rafters and dangle her there. But she did not ask. She could not speak. She could only marvel at him.

And Rasputin marveled at her, too. Why had she not died? He looked at her heart still beating strongly in his hat on the table, felt all her innards pressing in around him in his pockets, pulsing and quickening and writhing. But it was only a matter of time. She thought he was magical, had magical powers, but she was fooled, this fat girl with yellow eyes.

"Levitate me," she said at last.

"I can't."

The fat girl frowned. "I'm too heavy," she said.

"No," Rasputin said. "You think you know me? Ha! Why? Because of the tricks?"

"Yes," she said. "They're not tricks."

"They are," he insisted. "You don't know anything."

The fat girl lay perfectly still inside the box. Her heart slowed in the hat on the table. Rasputin took off his coat. "Alright," he said. "Close your eyes."

The fat girl closed her yellow eyes, and Rasputin waved a hand over her hulking body lying expectantly inside the empty box of blades. He spoke some magic words. "Ali-ho-jeni! Kan-rupi! Tar-tuff!"

When she opened her eyes, he was gone. She looked down from the roof beams, through the struts and trusses, through powdered-up cobwebs and flue soot, through sea dregs and silica shimmering in the air. There was no painted wooden box, no red-handled sabers, no shards of glass. No magic wand, no crystal ball, no wilting rose.

No silk-lined cape, no split-tailed coat. No tall black hat.

No ticking watch. No lump of coal.

Run, Little Girl

Brother Harpy delivered serpents to their house, to her daddy, the minister of Lick Branch, who put them in the icebox so they'd grow sleepy enough to handle next day at church. "Takes just as much faith to reach into a bag of sleepy serpents," her father said, for the congregation was unaware, if she wasn't.

Brother Harpy caught snakes all over McDowell County, and every Saturday, she watched him pull into their dirt yard and unload sacks writhing with rattlers and adders and copperheads. When he handled them, the sacks twisted and hopped as vipers struck the sides of the bags, fangs sometimes snagging and poking through the burlap. Brother Harpy would untie a sack as she sat straddling the porch railing, swinging her long legs back and forth or painting her toenails with her mama on the steps. She and her mama would watch him reach inside the bag and bring out a cottonmouth the size of his forearm. The snake would strike and its fangs would catch in the cowhide and rubber sole of his boot.

Then he'd look over at her mama and her and smile, and they would smile back, couldn't help doing it, even though Brother Harpy didn't belong to church and everything about

67

him looked sinful. He was an old man, older even than her mama. His hair was down over his collar, almost as long as hers and had been dark once but now showed lots of gray, salt and pepper, her mama called it. He wore sunglasses and shirts with the sleeves torn off and a necklace of a kind that made him seem to have Indian in him, which is what they liked most about him, her mama and her. Something about the roughness of his face and the color of his skin, brown as a pear, made her think so, at least. He was an old, *old* man, but neither of them could take their eyes off him.

And he couldn't take his eyes off them either. Her mama was the sexiest woman in Lick Branch, had a body as good as her own only looked like she knew how to use it. Before she had firmly lost all faith, her mama had backslid six times. She was weak-minded, people thought. Weak willed. Spiritless. Of the flesh. Wicked, though none went so far as saying that. It stopped just short of that, for she was their pastor's wife.

Her daddy bore the shame of her mama's transgressions with humility and forgiveness. He forgave her her sins, he said, each evening. He was a meek and righteous man, and until she had reached a certain age, the girl had been his charismatic little angel, reaching into the burlap sack and drawing out diamondbacks and copperheads. Her child's faith convinced the sinners of Lick Branch that God would protect any who sought Him. She had saved many souls.

Including the soul of Elwood McGuire. When the news had reached Elwood McGuire about her, this young thing reaching into a sack of snakes and drawing them out and wrapping them about her arms and neck, when Elwood heard that, he had to see. And so he was drawn to the little white church he passed by every day, twice a day, on his way to the mines. He was drawn to the church and to the girl and to God Himself. And he became a great believer, picking her up under her arms and setting her up on the backs of pews where all could see her, this child of God.

And he traveled to churches and tent meetings far and wide, telling of her. Even when he got throat cancer and lost his real voice, took on that robotic voice of the tracheotomy, even then he praised God. And in a tent meeting over in Jolo, he took his leave, shouting and testifying. "Hal-le-lu-jah! I'm-a-be-liev-er."

The congregation had swollen up and stood on its feet, and each one had begun to fall away, each into his or her own spirit, some singing "How Great Thou Art," and others laying hands on Elwood, and still others speaking in tongues and shouting, their bodies no longer under their own control but filled with the Spirit of the Holy Ghost and moving about the tent wildly and falling to the dirt floor in convulsions, folks moving back metal chairs and making room so they would not hurt themselves too badly.

It was on this occasion that Elwood McGuire had been so fully filled with the Spirit and with a satisfied mind that he could have hugged and kissed the girl, that child who had drawn him into the bosom of Abraham. If she had been there at that particular tent revival that night. But she wasn't; she was home watching television, fanning flies with her mama. And so, he had shaken the hands of everyone in the congregation and stepped outside, his wet handkerchief not yet even pushed back into his hip pocket before he was run over by a Lick Branch Colliery coal truck, highballing down Bear Town Mountain, and killed.

* * *

There was something about him, Brother Harpy, something she couldn't name exactly, but something she felt and mostly at night, lying awake for hours the way she did, thinking back over her day. She'd heard he lived alone in a ramshackle, old company house somewhere near Johnnycake, and she wondered whether he could throw a tomahawk, and she guessed he could, that maybe he could kill a wildcat with one if he felt like it, or a snake.

She wanted to catch snakes herself, hot snakes with flicking tongues, angry serpents, not the sluggish pieces of rubber she'd handled at church. She felt she could, or at least she might have been able to at one time, when she was full of faith, before the coal truck and Elwood McGuire. You couldn't grab up snakes with fear and doubt in your heart. And that is what made her love Brother Harpy. He had no fear, and just looking at him, that slick hair, both dark and light at once, that rough-looking face with its dark eyes, made her feel something funny, something akin to courage, a boldness. She drew nearer and nearer to him when he came delivering snakes. She helped him carry the jumping sacks into the basement, and he did not warn her to be careful. "I ain't afraid," she said.

And he said, "You ain't, huh?"

She shook her head, and her blond hair fell down both sides of her face and moved like a soft breeze had picked it up and let it down again. He looked at her, standing under the single bulb of the hand-dug basement, her bare feet and calves gleaming white against the dark packed earth beneath them, her pretty pink toenails catching the light like opals. He tossed a sack into the basement and it jumped and rolled as the serpents fought each other inside the bag.

"How come they don't kill each other?" she said. And he told her he couldn't say. He stepped into the damp cellar and walked past her, picking up the sacks and throwing them into the icebox that was plugged into the same single light socket above their heads.

She had not flinched when the sack he'd thrown had flopped itself near to her, and he reached now to get it and throw it into the fridge. She stood still but the motion of his body caused the hem of her cotton dress to billow and lift slightly away from her legs. She pushed it down and he watched her and rose slowly, the sack still in his hand, and looked at her pretty face, her eyes so blue people had a hard time looking away from them, and so did he, she thought, staring back into his, which were dark and shiny, but not black. She couldn't tell what color they were, and she couldn't hold her gaze long enough to find out. She looked away first and smoothed her dress and stepped toward the door. "How old are you?" she said, and she saw his eyes lift from her hips to her face as she stepped away from him out into the light green of the day.

"How old do you think?" he said.

And she felt sassy, having caught his eyes where they'd been. "A hundred," she said. And he laughed, and his smile was a candle inside the dark cellar and his laughter a black boom.

When he came back outside, she was sitting on the tailgate of his truck, her legs swinging slowly, one then the other, then the one again and then the other. Her skin was the toughest it would ever be, soft as it looked, tough in its softness, for she could walk barefoot over sharp rocks and the skin of her feet would not break but stretch over them, like wax or clay that would then go back to its own shape again. He could see her knees now, too, and her legs parted slightly like a boy's, for she was a girl who hadn't yet made up her mind about what she wanted to be.

"You got Indian in you?" she asked when he stepped around the truck and threw the last batch of empty sacks he had retrieved from the cellar onto the floorboard. He came back around to her, leaned over the side of the truck and draped an arm inside no more than a foot away from her own bare arm. She turned to face him, drew one leg up onto the tailgate and settled it under her weight. "I bet you got Indian in you," she said.

He smiled at her again, but this time with no laughter, a different kind of smile, somber, more with his dark eyes than with his mouth, his face. And before she thought to look at his eyes again, to see their color, she fidgeted and hopped down from the bed of the truck, little pieces of weeds and dirt stuck to the backside of her dress. "What time is it?" she asked and looked at his wrist for a watch, but didn't see one there. "Don't you wear a watch?"

"Found none that'll run on my arm," he said.

"How come?" she said, and he looked at her with untelling eyes and rounded his shoulders. "Hmm," she said. He had tattoos on his arms, a long-stemmed rose on his right forearm and some kind of funny black design on the shoulder of his other one. "What's that mean?" she asked, but his eyes were drawn to something over her shoulder, her mama, standing on the porch watching them. She did not call to the girl, only stood holding onto the railing and looking. He walked toward the house, and the girl chased after him and ran around ahead of him and plopped down on the metal glider before he reached the porch.

He stood in the yard with one boot resting on the bottom step and the girl smiled broadly for having outrun him and breathed heavy, not trying at all to slow her breath, but breathing in and out hard like she was enjoying her lungs for the first time. Because a girl like that would not need to breathe so heavy after so short a run.

Her mama smiled at him, but he did not return the smile. He gave her mama a different look, a look the girl could not decipher. He parted his lips and the look seemed to emanate from there between the flesh of his lips, from somewhere inside his mouth and somewhere deeper, darker, wetter. Her mama held her daddy's wallet in her hands, the same thick brown leather of his belt, which had striped her legs and had even striped her mama's legs, maybe had striped her mama's legs even more than her own.

Her mama pulled money out of the wallet and handed it to him without counting it; whatever there was, she gave him. Then he smiled, that same full sober smile from the cellar, and took the money and folded it and lifted it to a make-believe brim of a hat he didn't wear. He nodded his gratitude, and looked again at the girl on the glider, rocking back and forth. He looked at her the same way another man had looked at her a couple of weeks earlier at the park when she had tried to ride a blue, iron pony she was too big for, her legs bent up like an insect's to fit in the mock stirrups. "Get up off that," her daddy had said, and given the man a bloodless look.

Her mama waited a minute more, as if there were something hanging between them to say, or as if maybe whatever it was had already been said, long ago, but not so very long. She looked at the girl, then, and turned to go, pulling open the screen door and pausing. The girl smiled at her, but her mama only half-smiled back, and then went inside without a word.

The girl walked across the porch and straddled the railing again, her dress hitched up high on her thighs, just barely higher than eye level where he stood at the bottom step. He looked at her long legs without apology and made no motion to go, though he had no more reason to stay now that he'd been paid by her mother.

"I bet your hands are fast," the girl said, snatching at the air and laughing. "And strong. To grab them snakes." She climbed down from the porch railing and came around to the steps where he stood, walked down to him and picked up his hand. She held his palm up and studied the lines. His hand was nearly as wide as half her body. She turned it over and rubbed her thumbs across the purple veins there. His hand was tan and warm, his fingernails slightly longish but clean, and she thought of a pocketknife somewhere amidst the fold of money he had shoved in his front pocket.

He was older than her daddy, but she wondered if he would kiss her if she kissed him first, and she guessed he would. She heard the fans blowing inside the house and longed for their breeze. It was hot there in the sun, but she knew a cool place, and she told him she did. She held onto his hand and pulled him into the woods, and he followed her, even when she turned loose and ran ahead again. He followed her.

They came down by a place in the river where the water ran fast over the rocks and shot through the exposed roots of gnarly, old oaks and ghost birches that grew out of the bank and leaned toward the sun. At the edge of the creek, she saw hoof marks and pointed them out. "Look," she said, her eyes already tracing the tracks farther down along the water and up the bank. She never saw them, she said, but they came there to drink. He stood watching her, unhurried, his gaze measured and exact. Just the sound of the water was enough to cool you, she told him. "It's colder than it looks, but we can go in if you want."

He only stood there, shook his head, but not with conviction. If she wanted to go in, he would.

But she didn't know what she wanted to do, only that she wanted to talk to him, to make him look at her, cause she liked that, how he looked at her. "I never showed nobody this place," she said, to have something say, "and here I bring a stranger to it. I don't even know you."

It was a question, a request. She wanted him to make himself known to her. "Has anybody ever told you, you look a little like the devil?" she said, smiling, not catching his eyes now because she was afraid to. "I think you *are* the devil," she said, walking around a tree and looking back at him. "That's how you catch them snakes, why you ain't afraid."

"And you ain't afraid either, huh?" he said, and something swept over his face, something ugly but it was too fast to tell what it was. Then he was smiling again, the most radiant he had smiled yet, and stepping toward her. "Kiss me," he said, taking her hand, pulling her to him. His body was warm; his arms folded around her like wings and warmed her.

"I shouldn't be here," she said, already tasting his kiss but pulling away.

"Kiss me," he said.

"I can't."

"One little kiss. It'll be fun. It'll be sweet. One little *cocktail* kiss."

It sounded funny, him saying cocktail, this snake catcher, and she realized she had no idea who he was, or where he came from, or what he wanted from her.

But he was so beautiful to her, like an angel, a dark angel, Lucifer himself, she thought, and she knew she should run, but she didn't want to.

"One little kiss," he supplicated, and his breath entered her mouth and settled on her tongue and it was as if she had already done it, kissed him, and so she did. She opened her mouth and let him come in, and it was like a scourge of demons had slithered inside her, his mouth upon hers so hard, his tongue darting deep inside. He pulled her long hair and twisted it around his fists and wrenched her neck to him. He lifted her off the ground and pressed her into the tree until her bare flesh was shorn by its bark. "Run, little girl," he said. And she knew if she did, he would only chase her down, grab her up with those big rough hands, and that's not what she wanted—to be caught. And anyway it was too late now, though her legs worked themselves as if she had willed them to, and that's what made her whimper, made him laugh. She would not be saved.

But she didn't care, because she loved him and she knew that he had never lied to her; somehow she had known it all along. He wasn't afraid of anything. Even if her father came, he wouldn't care. She opened her eyes and looked at him. They were eye to eye, and she saw their color at last. They were blue, his eyes. Blue as her own, but inky, double dyed, blue black like the wing of a wasp.

She smiled.

For what was happening now, her dress being ripped and shoved down over her body, his hips lifting and forcing her harder into the tree—all of it, everything, was entirely of her own doing.

Clinch

———

It had come a sudden shower. Water gushed down the mountains in raging gullies, turning the dirt roads into creek beds that fed into the tributaries of the Tug River. They clung to the care of the mountain, which offered up animal paths leading toward Clinch. The leaves of the trees rained down again as they passed beneath them, Dreama lifting the boughs of branches for the boys to hunker under. Across the river, they saw steam rising from the asphalt of US 52, the air now gathering heat and collecting on their foreheads.

Condy struggled under the weight of the crate he was carrying, the glass bottles clinking as he went. "Watch for pop tops when we get to the road," he called back. Willard had already cut his foot on one, coming out of the holler. They sauntered along, breaking up the twigs and the roots with their toughened little feet.

When they reached Slate Fork, Condy led the way down the steep embankment, balancing the crate before him, the muscles in his wiry forearms taut as baler twine. He touched bottom, then set down the wooden tote-box and reached up for Dreama to lower Willard by one arm. After Willard was safely over the swollen ditch, Dreama held fast to the saplings that would bend with her weight and lower her easily. They crossed over the swinging footbridge, muddy water churning below, and down toward the highway.

Though they didn't know it, the president was at that moment speaking to the nation from the campus of a university in Michigan. Elsewhere, there were protests and rumors of war, though none of it crossed the mountains that rose up on all sides and sheltered them.

In Clinch, they passed the depot and the coal tipple and a string of old company houses covered in tarpaper siding, perching precariously on foundations of stacked stones. Diesel fuel and the chuff of trains in the rail yard commingled with the smell of rain and earth and the twittering of birds scouring the ditches for worms. Willard slapped at the puddles and drove his toes deep into the warm black mud of the ruts and grooves alongside the road. He found a Nehi bottle, and turned, holding it high for Condy to see.

Across the river near the train trestle sat a Queen Anne–style mansion built by an early Pennsylvania coal baron on a street called Bosses' Row. Farther down the way sat the superintendent's home and the other big houses.

Roland Paynter's feed-and-seed store sat discordantly nestled in a row of new and old downtown merchants and offices. There was a furniture store and a funeral home. A bank, a barber, the post office. A burger joint and a five and dime had sprung up near the run-down movie theatre, where teenagers as far away as Mohawk had once come for the serials and still came occasionally for sock hops.

In the distance, rain hung in the sky like a swarm of bees, low and nebulous over the mountains, threatening a fresh downpour that might keep them waiting inside the feed store a long time. Roland's was one of the oldest structures in town, erected from sawmill slats harvested from virgin Appalachian timber, or so the stories told.

When they arrived, Dreama ushered the boys onto the porch where tin wall signs advertised Lark cigarettes and Royal Crown Cola. Water dripping from the eaves caught in the wind and speckled her face as she opened the screen door and shooed the boys inside. They had walked a long way, and Condy ducked under his mommy's arm to reach the cool, musty refuge within. He had carried the bottles clear from the head of Bramlick Holler, and he slid the yellow crate onto the scarred counter.

A TV was going in the far back corner of the store, and when the bell over the door rang, Roland's wife Donetta reached to turn it up. Dreama recognized the voice. It was the president speaking. He had just visited the area, was over in Inez, Kentucky, where he'd had his picture taken with lots of people in their yards. Dreama had liked him better for it, for displaying his ordinariness. She especially liked the one of him squatting down next to a man and his sons on their shabby front porch. Imagine, the president of the United States of America hunkering down in a crouch with his knees thrown wide open just like any other man would do.

"The challenge of the next half century," President Johnson was saying, "is whether we have the wisdom to use that wealth to enrich and elevate our national life, and to advance the quality of our American civilization."

Condy looked over his shoulder at his mother to see whether he should wait for Roland or Donetta to redeem the bottles for cash. He glanced toward the wire magazine rack under the small window, and decided the bottles would be alright if he left them alone there a minute.

"For in your time we have the opportunity to move not only

toward the rich society and the powerful society, but upward to
the Great Society."

Dreama inhaled slowly, the sweet scent of rotting cantaloupe
and the dry yeast of animal feed inundating her senses as she
paused to listen, a smile almost breaking at the corners of her
sunken mouth. She wore a loose-fitting housedress with a
reverse collar and big pockets, and looked to be about forty
years old though she was not yet twenty-eight. Her hair, nearly
three feet long, was wound into a small, hard knot at the base
of her skull and held tightly with bobby pins.

The screen door screeched open, stealing her attention, and
Herschel Seifert stepped inside. He was seeking reelection as
constable of Clinch, and Dreama supposed he was there to pass
out his customary bottle of whiskey for Roland's vote.

"Afternoon, Mrs. Paynter," he said to Donetta. "Boss
around?" He smiled, and Donetta called for Roland, who
entered the room carrying a case of baking soda.

Roland dropped the box on the floor at his feet and removed
his glasses to wipe at a speck of lint. "Put these sodi-powders
out," he barked at Donetta. "Back there on the dry-goods shelf."
He returned the horn-rims to the bridge of his nose and walked
across the room to shake hands with the constable. "Your
shipment came yesterday," he said, more brightly.

"Good," Seifert said, bellying up to have a look inside the
glass display case where Roland kept expensive pocketknives
and cigars and other specialty items.

Condy kept an eye on his bottles, thumbing absently
through the pages of a comic book, his daddy's old miner's
cap sliding over his eyes. He cocked the hat back and searched
for the letter column, running a finger down the page when
he found it.

Willard complained of the cut on his foot hurting, and
Dreama scooped him up and turned the toddler's thick ankle to

CLINCH 81

have a look. She rubbed spit on her fingers to wipe away some of the filth and then kissed the foot playfully again and again until Willard forgot the hurt and laughed. Then she latched him to her hipbone and made her way deeper into the dimly lit building.

The store was the nearest place in Clinch to shop if you didn't have a car. Or if you didn't have gas money to drive fifteen miles into Iaeger, which is where she usually went when Wannace could take her. There was a Piggly Wiggly in Massey, but that was clear across Huff County. Clinch was just a skip away from Johnnycake, and Johnnycake was just a skip away from Iaeger.

"The Great Society rests on abundance and liberty for all. It demands an end to poverty and racial injustice, to which we are totally committed in our time."

Seifert turned his attention to the television. "There's a true politician for you," he told Roland, gently pulling a silk handkerchief from his suit-coat pocket.

Roland slid a small door to one side and extracted a leather tobacco pouch, which he untied and rolled out on the flat surface of the counter. A couple of glass canisters of loose tobacco set on the shelf behind him, as well as several less expensive boxes of cigars, raw twists and plugs, and a large assortment of rolling papers and cans of snuff.

Seifert unfolded the handkerchief to reveal a hand-carved meerschaum pipe engraved in the image of a bearded old man. It was a beautiful pipe with a coppery patina just beginning to highlight the crags and crevices of the old man's beard. Seifert stuffed the handkerchief in his pocket, spun the pipe upside down, and tapped it against one palm to dislodge the old tobacco inside.

"Turn that racket off," Roland told Donetta, motioning toward the TV. She was bent over, reaching into the pasteboard box, her arms loaded with small cartons of baking soda, which she continued to shelve. Behind her a poster for Chesterfield Kings.

Dreama kept an eye on Condy as she rifled through a container of seed packets and then a box of sewing patterns. Thrown over her shoulder was a drawstring purse she'd made from a pattern Alma Riffe had given her. Dreama had not learned to sew expertly by hand, but she could piece together simple patterns.

Inside the purse were five booklets of pastel-colored food stamps, which she'd been receiving since January. One of her sisters in McDowell County had been getting stamps since the trial run Kennedy had initiated two years earlier. The miners' families in West Virginia had made an impression on the young senator when he'd come campaigning in 1960, and he had not forgotten them.

She bumped Willard down to the floor and steered him around stacked bags of Poulin Grain feeds and Purina bone meal, cracked corn and layer feed. They wound around tables of baler twine, stacks of galvanized washtubs, and a couple bins of moldering produce toward the shelves that stocked canned food items.

The wind picked up outside and slapped the screen door in its frame a couple of times, the little bell ringing wildly and then ceasing.

Seifert tossed the spent tobacco into the coal bucket beside the darkened potbellied stove behind him, and then leaned in close to inhale the new shipment's sweet pungency. He closed his eyes and breathed deeply, the corners of his graying mustache rising ever so slightly. "I don't generally care for the aromatics," he said, picking up a pinch of the tobacco and drawing it closer to take in its full effect. "But these Oriental blends make up for what they lack in flavor."

Roland smiled, nodding appreciatively. "You'll want to

smoke this one here slow. I'm told it'll start to burn hot if you smoke it too fast."

Condy came around from the other side of the counter and laid a hand on his bottles, the breeze through the screen door a welcome respite from the perspiration collecting under his arms and under his daddy's hat. He wanted to remind Roland that he had business to settle as well.

Roland followed the boy with his eyes, alert as an owl to his presence. "Go on now," he screeched, taking the boy aback. "I'll get your bottles when I take care of your mommy. She don't look ready to me. Does she you?"

Condy cut his eyes at the man. "I wasn't doing nothing," he said, sharply.

"Go on, now, I said. Get back there where your mommy can look after you."

Seifert packed the pipe with the new tobacco in stages, filling the bowl up and then tamping it down, repeating the process and drawing on the pipe to gauge how good a job he'd done. "Who you belong to?" he asked Condy. "What's your daddy's name?"

The boy's heart punched at his ribcage. He hadn't done anything to warrant such questioning.

Seifert waited for the boy to answer, not eyeing him directly. He struck a match and held the flame over the pipe, sucking in and moving the bowl in a circular motion until the fire spread evenly over the tobacco.

After a long pause, Condy squared his shoulders and spoke boldly. "Wannace Matney," he said, leveling his chin.

Seifert drew on his pipe, and then held it down where Condy could see its elaborate design. "I think it's a mountain man. What about you?"

Condy shrugged. "Maybe."

"Go on, take it," the constable said.

Condy wasn't sure whether the man meant for him to reach for the pipe and take a puff himself. He figured that's not what the man meant, so he simply admired it in the constable's outstretched hand. "I can see it fine here," the boy said. "Where'd you get it at?"

Seifert rose and drew the pipe to his lips again, taking another deep drag as he eyed Roland with a wink. "Got it at the getting place," Seifert said. "Special order from Turkey."

It was the finest-looking piece of handiwork Condy had ever seen, the carving more intricate than anything his paw-paw had ever whittled, and he was near expert with a pocketknife. Still, Condy withheld his appreciation of the pipe. He didn't like braggarts, even if they carried a badge. He would've liked to have seen that as well, the constable's badge, but he did not make mention of it. "You like my daddy's hat?" he said instead, lifting the old mining cap by the lip and tipping it at Seifert. "He got *it* at the getting place, too."

Seifert laughed and smoke seethed between his teeth, up and around the fancy pipe and into his hooded eyes. "Wannace Matney, you say?" He studied the boy's face. "You favor your mommy, I reckon then," he said with a chuckle. He pulled his wallet from his hip pocket and gave Condy a business card.

REELECT
CONSTABLE HERSCHEL SEIFERT
WARRIOR RIDGE DISTRICT #6

It had his picture on it and a phone number to his office at the municipal building. "Give that to your daddy, would you, honey?" he said, replacing the pipe in the corner of his mouth.

Condy slid the card into the pocket of his britches. "I ain't your honey," he said, this time more hatefully, and Seifert laughed again but not as much as before. "It don't make no difference if he votes or not."

Seifert held his politician smile a minute more. "Well, of course it does. Every red-blooded American ort to vote."

Dreama stepped into Condy's line of sight and motioned for him to come to her.

"I got to go," he said, and walked away from the counter toward his mother at the center of the store.

"That boy smart off to you?" Roland asked, stepping around the counter and following Condy with his eyes. "I never cared for a smart aleck. They drag in here from outen under a rock and sass every grown-up they see. They ain't taught no better."

"No," Seifert said. "I guess they ain't."

Condy eyed the few dusty boxes of cereal and the lunch-meat counter where he'd seen Roland slice rolls of bologna and wrap it in thick sheets of white paper. He knew the store better than his mother did, for he was ambitious in his efforts of collecting bottles.

"Don't you be talking to nobody like that," Dreama scolded quietly when he reached her.

"Wasn't aiming to," he said.

"Stay back here." She pulled him close and ushered him away from the men. "Is there anything special you want?"

He paused a moment and nodded, then walked with purpose to the ice-cream freezer. "Up here, Mommy," he said, sliding back the cooler door and lowering his head so that a stream of cold white air rolled up over his sweaty face and bare shoulders.

She'd promised them a treat.

"It's called a television dinner," Condy said, holding up a thin rectangular package that showed the contents inside: peas, mashed potatoes, and Salisbury steak served in a little tinfoil tray that could be heated in the oven.

"I thought you was going for an ice-cream sandwich," Dreama said. "You want *peas*? I got peas put away in the cellar. I never heard tell of no television dinners." She smiled without showing her teeth, her eyes doing the smiling for her.

"You eat them in the living room, watching TV," Condy explained. The shine in the apples of his cheeks made her want to bite on them the way she'd done when he was a baby. He had not let her love on him like that in two or three years. He was too big for her affection now, and she found herself studying him lately like the tadpoles he kept watch over in the muddy shoals of the creek. A couple times a week she left Willard at the house with Wannace while she hitched up the tail of her dress and climbed down over the rock wall to look with her eldest son for signs of things changing.

"How much is it?" she asked.

"Ain't but eighty-nine cent. I can buy it myself if they ever pay me for my bottles."

"Eighty-nine cent seems high for a spoonful of peas and—what's that say? *Chilled Meat?*"

She lifted Willard and he clung to her like a June bug. "How about you, baby? You want you some chilled meat in one of them television dinners? Or had you rather have you a bar of candy?"

"Candy!" Willard cried, his little bare chest and legs blackened from playing hard in the retreads Wannace had thrown out beside the house. She swept him up in her arms and gnawed on his fat cheeks, and Willard squealed with laughter. "Stop it, Mommy! That tickles," he said, his pretty baby teeth gleaming.

"Run pick you out something," she said, setting him down and swatting him on the backside as he scrambled toward the candy rack.

Condy stood reading the label of the package in his hands. "Convenient and nutritious," it said.

Dreama removed Wannace's miner's cap from his head and rubbed her hand over the velvet softness of his buzz cut. "Don't this old thing get hot?"

He smiled, shaking his head no, showing the new tooth that had gone bad. Then he ran off to search for a *Fightin' Army* comic to buy with the money he would earn from his bottles.

"A third place to build the Great Society is in the classrooms of America. There your children's lives will be shaped. Our society will not be great until every young mind is set free to scan the farthest reaches of thought and imagination."

Such words, Dreama thought, turning to catch a glimpse of the TV. Donetta stood watching again, a lime-green polyester blouse revealing her bra straps beneath, cutting into her flesh and quartering her like a shoulder of beef. There was LBJ on the screen, a big man, ordinary looking, ordinary talking. And here he was stirring something inside her. What was it? She thought of her mommy meeting President Kennedy over in Welch, the prettiest man her mommy said she'd ever seen, shaking his hand, looking him in his Irish eyes, and moved to believe his promises.

"Poverty must not be a bar to learning, and learning must offer an escape from poverty."

Roland glared at Donetta and looked again at the TV. Dreama picked up a five-pound bag of pintos and then set them back when Donetta snapped the television off suddenly, cutting off the president midsentence. The tube inside it sparked white and faded like a slowly dying lightning bug.

Donetta ran her eyes over the boys, taking in their bare backs and feet, then looked at Dreama with a pickled old face. Dreama lowered her eyes to the rough planks of the floorboards, and just like that the good feeling she was having was yanked away like a bad tooth.

There wasn't much to choose from at Roland's except the usual fare. Maybe she would go into Oxbow or Iaeger down in McDowell County later on for some kind of meat. She might find pork chops at the Piggly Wiggly. They hadn't had meat in ages, she realized. Nothing except the occasional chicken her daddy had given them when she'd gone checking on him. Wannace hated chickens, thought they were nasty, or else she would've put a few out in the yard to roost in the trees the way her mommy had done. Dreama and her sisters had made a game of searching for the eggs, though she, being the youngest, had always been scared of broody hens, for they pecked her hands when she tried to reach under them. Her mommy had traded and collected different breeds from all over the county. Some had muffs on their faces that looked like beards or furry spurs on their legs that looked like they were wearing Eskimo boots. She had liked watching them peck and scratch for food, the rooster always calling the others to come and eat first, picking up the feed and dropping it until the hens flocked around.

She picked up the beans again and checked the price of a jar of instant coffee, ninety-nine cents. She needed flour, too, forty-nine cents, and washing powders, fifty-nine, though that kind of stuff couldn't be bought with stamps. She would love to have bacon, but it was too steep. She kept a tally in her head, cradling as much as she could carry in her arms and making her way to the counter where Roland stood waiting for her. The constable had poured what was left of the fancy tobacco in his drawstring pouch and stepped outside on the porch to wait out the rain. Dreama searched around for the children and called them to her.

Roland pressed the No Sale button on the register and took out forty-eight cents. He was an imposing man, looming large above the counter, with an air Dreama couldn't always read. He wore a necktie under an apron rubbed with dirt where he had lifted bags of animal feed and spud potatoes. He handed the coins to Condy, who looked at his mother with a question on his face.

"Go on," she said, "you earn't it." And he knew it was okay to choose something to spend the money on. He had been eyeing the comic book, but he might well prefer a pack of BBs from the dime store. He had shot up his last playing army with his buddy.

"I'll need taters," Dreama said. "Can you empty that peck into a sack?" Roland nodded. "Lard, too," she added, as he punched up all the numbers on the till. When he'd finished, he reached under the counter and brought out her credit tab and commenced to refiguring her debt.

"Just this here," she said. "How much?"

She'd added four cans of tuna in place of meat, a jar of mayonnaise, a bag of onions, cornmeal, and a quart of buttermilk. The till said six dollars and forty-two cents. She reached into her purse and pulled out one book of food stamps. She counted out seven stamps worth a dollar apiece and tore them carefully from the booklet. Then she counted out twelve more to settle her previous debt and slid them across the counter.

"That's the cash price," Roland said, thumbing his glasses further up the bridge of his nose. "It's a lot of rigmarole to fool with the federal government."

"You got a sign up says you accept food stamps," Dreama said.

Roland ignored the comment, stooping and pulling a small box from beneath the counter. He set about refilling a display rack with Tug-O'-War Plug tobacco as if he didn't care one way or the other if she bought the groceries.

"Me and Wannace been coming here nine or ten year," she said, raising her voice and looking to Donetta now for parity.

The constable looked inside from the porch to see what was the matter, but he did not offer to do anything.

The old grocer rested his hands on the counter and drummed his fingers. "'Preciate your business."

When Dreama saw that Donetta had no intention of disputing her husband, she asked sharply, "Wull, how much is it then?"

Roland opened a jackknife and cut himself a piece of plug tobacco to chew. "Double," he said, pushing the plug deep into the pocket of his jaw and working it with his false teeth.

"Double?" Dreama said. "My God, don't the rich get richer." Her anger caused her eyes to dart from one face to another and then back at the groceries spread over the counter. She considered returning the onions to the produce bin. She had recently put out lettuce and onion sets in the garden, but they wouldn't be big enough to eat for months. She heaved a sigh and rooted around inside her purse for more stamps.

Condy eased around his mother and slid the TV dinner off the counter. "I'll get one next time," he said.

"You leave that alone," Dreama growled, trapping the box where it set on the counter.

"I don't want it now," he said, making a hard show of his feelings toward Roland.

Willard's face was covered in chocolate. He pressed into Dreama's thigh and wrapped his arms around her legs. She ripped out more food stamps and shoved them across the counter.

"Grab them taters," she told Condy. She took up the five-gallon bucket of lard by the handle and wrapped her other arm around the brown bag of groceries.

Roland leaned over the counter, unwrapping a chocolate bar and waving it at Willard. The child's face lit up, and he reached for the dangling lure.

Dreama's expression folded in on itself in disbelief. What was that old cuss doing now?

Roland placed the candy in Willard's upturned palm and then lifted his eyes back to Dreama. She exhaled angrily and set down her bag to reach inside her purse again.

"No charge," he said.

She was perplexed, then she was mad again, and then she was ashamed, though she couldn't say why.

"That youngin' there's got the worms," Donetta said, directing her comment at Roland but in a voice loud enough for Dreama and Condy to hear. "I'll guarantee it."

Dreama's nostrils flared. She picked up the handle of the lard bucket, drawing the brown bag up into the crook of her free arm and lowering her eyes. She didn't trust that she could gaze upon either of them another second without there being some trouble.

Condy steered Willard by the shoulder to where she stood. Then he hoisted up the burlap bag of potatoes and balanced it on his left shoulder.

"Let's go," Dreama said. "H'it's a long walk home."

Little Miss Bobcat

———

For school-pride week, I wore my angel-wing dress and drew one of the best, if not *the* best, bobcats in my whole class. Mr. Munger taped the real pretty ones, like mine, on our classroom door. Needy Baker's drawing got put on the door, too, but hers wasn't nearly as good as mine and Lester Luster's. Lester's was mean looking with sharp teeth showing and one paw scratching at the air. It was good for a boy. But mine was more real looking. Everybody knows a bobcat looks mostly like a real cat, except they're a little bigger and have long sideburns like Elvis. I made mine with long sideburns, but not like Elvis's. I made them more like Abraham Lincoln's. Mine wasn't smiling like some people's were, but it wasn't mean either. It was just serious, like a cat is.

I have always been a good artist. I can look at something and color it exactly the way it is. If I color a butterfly, for instance, I use black and yellow. I have never seen a purple or pink butterfly in my entire life.

After we drew our bobcats and napped for a little while on our towels, Mr. Munger sent Lester Luster and me to the cafeteria to pick up the afternoon ice-cream order. We have ice cream every Wednesday, and sometimes I get a strawberry cup or an orange Push-Up, and sometimes I don't get anything. It depends on how much money I find in Daddy's wallet. Daddy's pants are always laying on the floor beside the bed, so I usually sneak in and check before I ask, but there wasn't no need to that morning. I didn't feel like ice cream anyway. I erased the boards until everyone was through and then Mr. Munger let any of us who wanted to sign up for the Little Miss Bobcat contest. "Whoever gets the most donations in a month," he said, "will win a genuine quartz crown and will get to ride on the Bobcat Grammar School float in the Easter parade."

I could already see myself up there in my angel-wing dress and my big Little Miss Bobcat crown, waving at everybody just like Miss America. I practiced by raising my arms out to my sides so my angel wings would hang down. You could see my arms inside the see-through purple cloth, so I was wondering if I could maybe wear long gloves, too, like Miss America does. Then all of a sudden, Needy Baker told everybody my panties were showing. "Why don't you wear something that fits you sometime?" she said. "And why don't you comb that hairy head of yours?"

I ran my hand down the back of my hair and it was still as smooth as when I'd left that morning. My hair is just thick, not long and slick like Needy's. I didn't say anything back. I knew she was just jealous. Then she told me to stick out my hands and show everybody what old-lady skin I have. "She's got a fungus. Don't touch her," she said. All of a sudden, I wished my sleeves weren't see-through anymore. My arm itched, but I didn't scratch it. I just took a parent sign-up sheet from Mr. Munger and went back to my seat, making sure to swipe the back of my dress tight before I sat down. Beth Blankenship,

Mr. Munger's pet, smiled at me, but I wasn't tricked. She always asked me what I made on tests and smiled like that. I drew her face just the way it was—mean.

One of the reasons I am so good at seeing things how they really are is because I watch *Mr. Rogers* every day. Mr. Rogers says you can tell how someone is feeling by their face. You can look at their eyebrows and eyes and mouth. For instance, you can tell my mommy is aggravated a lot by the places she digs on her neck.

Mr. Rogers is my favorite show, but when I got home that day Linda Anne was humped up in my chair watching *Romper Room*. "Why you got that on?" I asked, even though she already knew I can't stand that show and I shouldn't have to say anything. But she's stopped minding me. Anybody can see the magic mirror isn't real. "Look how fake," I said. "That woman can't really see us through the TV. How dumb." I like the Neighborhood of Make Believe better because it comes right out and tells you it's just pretend.

"Who said you can be in my chair anyway?" I went on, pulling Linda Anne by the arm.

"I was here first," she said. "Daddy says whoever is first can have it." She fell deadweight against me.

"Well, this ain't your daddy's house. And this chair ain't his either. That television, this living room, everything belongs to us." I stopped right there and turned loose because I thought I heard a grown-up coming. Sometimes I wish I did have a magic boomerang. I'd wave it and make Linda Anne's whole family and the other one that's piled in on top of us just disappear. Mommy and Daddy have got enough worries without all these others to take care of. I am the only good thing in their life.

The first thing I do every morning is start toeing everybody sleeping all over the house to get up. Then I pick up all the pallets and put up all the blankets and pillows that are strewn everywhere. We cannot stand a mucked-up house. I also keep all of the kids out from under Mommy's face, except for the ones older than me, who won't mind a lick.

At school, I make all Hs and H+s, which means highest achievement. Last year, Daddy gave me a dollar for every one I made, which wound up being ten dollars and a roll of quarters, which I didn't like spending. This year I said I'm too big for that, but he says I'll still get every dollar I'm due. This makes me worry whether I should do as good as before. Even though Daddy's a real good mechanic, the only motor in our yard right now is our own, swinging from a motor mount I helped build out of some trees we skinned the bark off of. Lately, Daddy's took to running around with Ronnie Hurley, our landlord, and stays away as long as possible because Mommy takes out all her frustration on him. She is still mad at him for having to break her mushroom ashtray over his head.

I tried to forget about all that for a while, though. Instead, I thought of how Mommy and Daddy would love to have something new to brag on me about. I am their pride and joy. Mommy sings that song to me all the time. *You're my pride and joy!*

I made a beeline to the kitchen, where she could help me make my donation bank. She's real good at doing things up. I asked her could I have a gallon mayonnaise jar to make it out of. "Best reason I can think of for running out," she said. But then she turned me around by my arm and looked at my head. "Go get me the hairbrush," she snapped. I didn't sass. I did as I was told and let her jerk my brains out until she was satisfied. My hair is just real thick. Then I brought up the contest again, and after that she rinsed out the mayonnaise jar and dried it. Then she took a butter knife and scraped the label off. "Here. Practice your cursive." She handed me a light bill envelope to write on. I didn't know how to spell donations, but Mommy did. She was going to be a teacher when she grew up, but she took the wrong Chevy Nova out of York, Pennsylvania, or something like that.

Anyway, then she sheared off the edges of the light bill and stuck my sign to the jar by smearing the back of it with canned cream. Cream is like a miracle glue. I've seen her fix dozens of ashtrays with it. After that, we decorated the jar with macaroni and sugar and blue and red food coloring while we sang along with Elvis on our floor-model stereo.

I danced while she smoked a cigarette and worked and sung at the same time. I can do the Charleston a little bit but not as good as Mommy, and anyway you couldn't do the Charleston to Elvis. Mommy sings even better than Patsy Cline and is prettier, too. She looks just like the lady in *I Dream of Jeanie*, everybody says. I tried Mommy's dances, the pony and then the jerk, but finally I just twirled my arms over my head and hummed.

All of a sudden, Mommy looked up at me and quit singing. She rested her cigarette on the edge of the table. "Beatrice, I want you to give that dress to one of your cousins," she said. "Let Linda Anne try it on."

"No, Mommy," I begged.

"You heard me." She'd been making me a paper crown, too, and after she dusted the unstuck sugar off it, she wedged it on my head. My bangs mooshed down into my eyes. "I should've known it'd be too little," she said. Then she wadded up all the newspaper and wiped down the table with a rag.

"It's not too little," I said, pulling the crown further down on my head so that it ripped a little bit, even though I pretended that it didn't. "I don't want to give it to Linda Anne," I tried again. Mommy took up the cigarette and leaned against the sink just looking at me. She found a little place on her face she didn't like and started scratching.

I folded up my angel wings and breathed through my mouth to keep my head little.

* * *

The first person I hit up for a donation was Uncle Oliver, Linda Anne's dad. "Honey, you know how poor old Uncle Ollie is," he said. Like he was proud of it.

"You don't even have a quarter?" I said. "Not even a penny? Even a penny would help me win."

"Vainglory," he said. "Vaaainnnglory."

I don't understand much of what Uncle Oliver talks about, and I can't ever tell what his face is feeling either. He smiles all the time and it's not a mean smile like Beth Blankenship's, but I don't know what it is.

Daddy walked in the front door and headed for the kitchen. A little while later, Mommy's voice raised and drifted into the living room with Uncle Oliver and me.

"That's all I have," she said.

"I'll get more."

"When? I need it."

"I'll go to Sydney's this week." Daddy walked back through the living room carrying a plastic baggie full of salt.

"Some old wives' tale," Mommy yelled at him. She slid an iron frying pan across the oven rack and it sounded like thunder coming over the mountain. "Pretty soon we won't have lights or salt!" She slammed the oven door and we heard it bounce back open a little. I figured her spoon collection would hit the floor, but it didn't.

Daddy walked outside and I followed him to see if I could help sort screws and bolts and to tell him about Little Miss Bobcat, but he was busy. We walked around behind the house and Daddy held down the briars for me. Then he set the bag of salt on the meter box and tapped the glass to see if it had slowed any.

"Contests ain't nothing but scams," he said, plodding over toward his work shed.

"I'll get a crown," I said. "A real one." A tree limb raked crumbs of sugar into my eye from the one Mommy'd made me. I should've made it myself, I thought. I could've drawn diamonds on it.

Daddy just looked at me funny. "Bring your bank out here Friday night," he said, unrolling a piece of black tarpaper with his big square hands. He measured the side of the building and then cut the tarpaper with his pocketknife. "Run in and grab a handful of roofing nails."

I know just which ones are roofing nails. They're short and have the fat tops. I set my donation bank down on the ground and climbed up into Daddy's work shed, which has no steps and is a little high off the ground. I got some dirt on my body suit when I crawled up in the building on my belly. I felt the snaps give, too, and I was kind of glad, 'cause they were cutting off my circulation anyway. Daddy's workshop is real neat inside with little plastic bins for everything, homemade boxes and Bama jelly jars full of all kinds of nails and screws and washers and bolts. I unfastened a jar and shook out as many nails as I could hold in one hand. Then I twisted it back into the lid mounted under a shelf.

Outside, Daddy ran the tarpaper up over the windows and nailed it in place. I helped him wrap the whole shed and then we found a padlock and bolted the door shut.

*   *   *

My donation jar stayed pretty empty for the first few days because Mommy wouldn't let me walk up into the hollers by myself. I asked could I go with my teenage cousins, even though I knew they wouldn't look after me and that some big dog might eat me up. Mommy ain't dumb. "No," she said.

Later on, we wound up going to Corbin's Phillips 66 station in Iaeger. I raked it in there because Corbin pestered anybody who turned me down till they were so ashamed they finally stuck a dollar in my jar. Corbin himself gave me ten dollars, but then he said, "You ought to just keep whatever money you get. Can't win no way. Them Bakers got it all sewed up."

I hadn't thought about keeping the money till then. I could buy some clip-on roller skates, maybe even a baton, things I needed. I could buy Mommy a lace angel doily. But then I realized Corbin was only testing me. "Nuh uh," I said, quick, knowing it made Mommy and Daddy proud that I was so honest. Still, I wondered if Corbin was right about Needy's family. But that only made me want to win even more, to prove a point.

* * *

As the money started adding up, I realized how careful I had to be. My one cousin was dropping out of high school to have a baby, who would need a crib and diapers. "Somebody explain to me how this is going to work," Mommy said, looking straight at Uncle Oliver. "I tried to get y'all to put that one on birth control pills, didn't I? But no."

I counted every penny twice a day and kept a running total on the bottom of my shoe, so no one could trick me. I sat on the porch, watching the coal trucks pound their way down the hairpin curve around our house, holding my jar instead of Drowsy, who Linda Anne now claimed, slinging her around by the string that used to make her talk. "I'm sleepy," she used to say, or "Bring me another drink of water." Her face never changed from being happy and tired.

After I hid my jar, I went to see if there was anything I could help Daddy with. He's a real good mechanic. Better than them at the Swift Lube where everybody likes going, all of a sudden.

Whenever he needs gas to soak parts in, I know how to siphon some from the Nova just like he does. You have to keep your head low to the ground and puff till you feel the gas kind of pull up and hold at the top of the hose. I'm good at drawing it up, but I'm not too quick yet with the milk jug. I still get it in my mouth sometimes. It burns and Mommy complains that I'm going to turn my lips all inside out.

Daddy was on his way to Sydney's for groceries, and I decided to go, too. I figured I could hit Sydney up for a donation. His store is a two-story building with groceries on the bottom and feed-and-seed stuff upstairs. I like the big round wheels of cheese on the counter. But we never buy that. We always get the same things: ten pound bags of sugar, flour and pintos, a five-gallon bucket of lard, and fifty pounds of potatoes. These used to last us a long time, but lately Daddy has started going to Sydney's every time you turn around. I hadn't been in a while, and I remembered Daddy's wallet and wondered how we were going to pay for our stuff.

Since the Nova wasn't running, Daddy and I walked through the pasture to Ronnie and Claire's trailer to see whether they would let us borrow their van. Daddy was being quiet because my uncle on Mommy's side, Uncle Hume, had whipped his daughter real hard and left stripes all over her. She is one of the teenagers. She snuck up into Long Pole and got drunk with some boys. "You want to wind up pregnant, too?" he hollered and then took off his belt. When Mommy thought he'd done enough, she pulled a butcher knife on him and he started crying like a drunkard. Then he told Mommy he was sorry and she threw the knife in the sink and said, "I am losing my mind."

When we got to Ronnie and Claire's yard, their big dog knocked me down and skinned up my knees. I was already not too crazy about Ronnie and Claire because they bring their fights over into our yard at all hours of the night. I was a little scared about riding in their van, too. Ronnie revs its engine up and threatens to drive through our house if Mommy doesn't tell him where Claire is hiding. He always thinks she's with us, but she isn't.

Daddy knocked on their ripped-up screen door and Claire answered. I asked her for a donation and she dug me up some change from her macramé pocketbook. I know not to look at her glass eye, so I concentrated hard as I could on the other one while I was talking. It's real hard to do, though, especially because I wanted so bad to see if I could tell what her face was feeling. But common sense says she must be sad to have a glass eye.

After Daddy asked Ronnie could we borrow his van, we drove over to Roderfield where Sydney's is. I was real excited about asking Sydney for a donation, and I gave him my speech about helping our schools. "School pride," I said. Then I heaved my big jar of money up onto the counter.

"Lot of money you got there, gal."

"Hundred and seven dollars and seventy-three cents," I said, smiling. I cocked my crown back and felt it rip even more than before, which upset me but only a little since I figured I'd soon be giving it to Linda Anne anyway.

Sydney looked over his flyspecked glasses at Daddy.

"Go out to the van, Beatrice," Daddy told me. I moved out of the way but didn't leave. Sydney took out a pad and wrote down everything we got, which this time included a roll of bologna and cheese and four loaves of Wonder Bread in the polka-dotted wrapper.

"We got everything?" Daddy asked me, and Sydney's eyes fell on me as if to say, "What else do you all want?" I said yes, even though I knew we were forgetting Mommy's salt. I would like to draw the little girl on the saltbox, but I didn't think about it at the time. I looked at Sydney's face and didn't like how small his eyes were. Shining through his thick glasses, they looked like they were set deep into his head, and they wiggled like something does that's underwater. I didn't look at Daddy's eyes. Common sense said not to. Instead, I looked down into my jar of money and thought about sticking my hand inside and turning over what we owed. I didn't want Daddy to be ashamed, though. I twisted the lid tight for Sydney to see. Soon our name would sparkle like the Little Miss Bobcat crown. I'd show them every one.

* * *

That Friday night, I carried my donation bank out to Daddy's work shed, where he and some other men were playing cards. I knew Ronnie, of course, and Lester Luster's dad, Jerry Dean, but not anyone else. They looked me up and down with mean eyes. "Send your kid out here to clean us out?" they joked, like I was bumming money instead of working for it.

Uncle Hume had wanted to play too but Daddy said it didn't make sense to play against each other. "Double our luck," Uncle Hume said. But Daddy said it would only half it and Uncle Hume got mad. "Alright, big shot," he said.

Uncle Oliver had snuck in behind me. Daddy didn't like it, I could tell, but he didn't say anything. "Come to sit one in, Ollie?" he asked, turning up his coffee cup.

"Got no need for money. God provides." I didn't know how Uncle Oliver could stand there without being ashamed of himself. Linda Anne didn't own a rag Mommy hadn't made me give her. And what I'd given her never looked the same on her as it had me. She wore it all poor. I could just see my fancy angel-wing dress hanging on her all slouchy.

"We'll take food stamps, Oliver," one of the men I didn't know said, laughing. I looked at the center of the card table, and two pink booklets were already mixed in with the money. I wondered if these had been Lester's dad, Jerry Dean's, but I couldn't picture it. Not a proud man like that.

"I'll give you a buck to run in and get me a cup of coffee," Daddy said, winking at me. He whispered something in my ear while the other men watched us, smiling. "Float me a loan and I'll triple your money," Daddy told me. Then to the grinning men playing cards he said, "Okay, boys, listen up. My little girl's trying to win a crown at school. Now who wants her to fetch some cold pop and sandwiches for a small donation?" Daddy winked at me again and then took hold of my bank. "I'm going to cash in some of these ones for you, honey." His hands were bigger than the mouth of the jug, so he turned it up and shook out a wad of bills. "Tell your mommy to give you a fifty when you go inside, okay?"

I imagined how fat all that money would've made Daddy's wallet. "What's it going toward, there, little miss?" one man asked, and I either couldn't remember or had never really known. I shrugged. I was too worried about Daddy's big hands fishing out all the dollars I'd saved to care about making any more money. "I guess it don't really matter," the man said, handing me a quarter.

"Don't be such a cheapskate," Jerry Dean told the other man. "Here. I'll take two sandwiches with lettuce and tomato and a little bit of salt. Nothing else." He handed me two dollars.

"You get that, Beatrice?" Daddy asked me, sorting my money and stacking it in piles. He left the change and a few bills inside and then slid the jar back to me. There sat almost all of my donations. What if he lost it? Needy Baker would beat me and then everybody would laugh at us.

"But Daddy," I said, staring down into the jar and then at the money stacked between his elbows. The men around the poker table looked at me like they were afraid I was going to start crying.

"What's wrong?" Ronnie said, like I was a baby. I cut my eyes at him. Then they all started snickering and looking at each other. Even Lester's daddy Jerry Dean leaned over his hand of cards, laughing to himself. He dropped his Lucky Strike in a pop bottle and the smoke swirled around before the drop of orange Crush put the fire out.

"Go on, Beatrice," Daddy said. He didn't understand why I wanted to win so much or what it felt like to be laughed at, but I couldn't risk letting him lose my money. I started to say something else, but he slapped his coffee cup down in my hand real hard so that I couldn't help from mouthing an *o-o-w*! I knew it showed on my face because Jerry Dean and the other men shook their heads and clucked their tongues at Daddy, like they were his mommy or something. I knew what they were doing, laughing at me but acting like they were trying hard not to. I would make a good poker player—I read their faces like it wasn't nothing.

"That's my school money," I finally said, crossing my arms over my chest. This was what Daddy really wanted, I knew, because he sat there smiling at me, his eyes all shiny with pride, his face blushing red.

I was thinking of what else I could do to show old Jerry Dean and Ronnie how smart and good I was. I started singing "On a Hill Far Away," but before I got to "there's an old Chevrolet," Daddy all at once yelled at me.

"Go and get the damn coffee, Beatrice, like I told you. We're in the middle of a game." What was he yelling at *me* for? I jerked when he'd done that and felt the crown rip further up the back of my head. Daddy's eyes were watering so much from all the cigarette smoke that they were soupy. He looked at the fellas sitting around the table and everyone shut up and studied their stacks of money and food stamps. Jerry Dean shuffled the deck, breaking the cards and slapping them back together over and over before he finished. Then he dealt the first card down and the next one up.

"You in?" he asked, holding the next card out. Everyone was quiet. I held my breath to keep my head little. Jerry Dean waved the playing card again. Daddy let out a long quiet breath and folded.

Merope

This old girl wasn't much to look at, but she took a shine to me that wore me down after a while. I shouldn't have done her like I did, but hell, we were just kids.

I had me a little twenty-two rifle my daddy had give me one birthday, and me and some buddies had built us a deer stand out in the woods near my uncle Estil's place. She was plain, this girl, but she had a cousin that tore me up. Jessica was the cousin's name. Gorgeous. Wore them bandolier tube halters with the string that run up around her neck. Kept me in fits two summers in a row.

This other one though was just a skinny-assed kid that brought cookies and cold pops to me out on the ball field. Wrote me a couple of poems. Sweet old girl, really. Took to following me around like a damned cat. My buddies got to ribbing on me for how homely she was, and that right there's when I should have said something. Should have shut it down right there. But like I said, we were all just kids, messing around.

I had a dirt bike in them days, little Yamaha 125 with the mufflers sawed off. That thing would scream. This old girl, I forget her name now, come knocking on the back door one evening about suppertime. Asked Mama could she speak to me in the backyard, where our houses butted up neighbor to neighbor. I'd run, hid in the laundry room, told Mama to get rid of her. Only she scolded me into speaking to the girl like somebody with sense.

We sat on the picnic table and leaned back after a while to look up at the stars. It was dark out and she had a pretty voice I'd never noticed before. She knew the names of the stars and the stories that went with them. I didn't know they had stories, but she told them to me. The one I remember best is about the hunter, Orion. She said the legends were sometimes mixed up, but the version she liked best, and the one she told me, was the one where the hunter could walk on water. He was the handsomest man on earth and he walked across the sea and met a goddess named Merope. Merope's father didn't like Orion and wouldn't let them be together. Orion got pissed and threatened to kill every beast on the earth, and then he got drunk and attacked Merope.

She was a good storyteller, that old girl was. We laid there on the picnic table looking up at Orion's hunting dogs, Canis Major and Canis Minor, and then she reached over and took my hand. And I let her. I don't know why I did it, but I felt myself turning toward her then and reaching out to touch her face in the dark. I had always been drawn to the pretty ones, but I saw something pretty in her that night while the starry summer sky loomed large over us. There was a little tremble in her cheek when I touched it that made me feel big. I kissed her and her hair smelled pretty and I wished for a minute it wouldn't turn light out, that the night would cover us and keep us that way.

But then I thought of my buddies and I shrunk back to the badass I thought I was. I wiped my mouth with the back of my hand and rose to go inside. "That kiss there was for your cousin Jessica," I said. "Tell her to come and see me sometime."

I couldn't see the hurt on her face, but I knew it was there. Stupid shit we do when we're kids, cruel shit, and we don't even know why.

* * *

Some weeks later, I saw her walking home from the store with a heavy brown tote bag and pulled up beside her on my dirt bike. I wasn't supposed to be riding it on the road, but the law never came out that way and Daddy didn't care. "Hop on," I told her. "I'll give you a ride home."

"Ain't going home," she said. "Taking this to Grammaw's."

"She lives over by Uncle Estil, don't she? Hop on. I'm going right by there."

She looked down at her tennis shoes. "It's not that far," she said. "I'll walk."

"Don't be like that now," I said. "Come on. Show me some mercy."

She studied my face for lies and there was a shine in her eyes. It about burned me, that shine. I swallowed, and she climbed on behind me and wrapped an arm around my waist and pressed the tote bag between us. I kick-started the dirt bike and revved the gas so the noise would cut through the burn I was feeling everywhere, and we let out of there not speaking the whole distance.

"You want to take a walk later?" I asked when we got there. I pushed her hair out of her face, and it was kind of growing on me, her face. It was small and fine boned and there was a dimple, high on her cheek just under her eye when she smiled. There wasn't anything special about her until you looked at her close like that. And that was the damnedest thing about that old girl. It felt like my eyes is what were doing the changing.

"I'd like that a lot," she said, smiling behind her lips, that dimple rising up like a star in the night sky.

We walked through Uncle Estil's Burley tobacco fields toward the woods where I'd been fattening up deer on apples Daddy and me got me from the co-ops. The 'bakker had already been harvested and left standing on full stalks turned upside down in the fields to wilt. It looked like hundreds of little teepees. Like we had stepped back in time.

I carried a bag of Rome Beauties in one hand and laced my fingers through hers with my other. When we got to the start of the path, we stopped and I cut an apple in half and rubbed it on the bottoms of both our shoes so the deer would be lured to the place where my deer stand was perched high in a big white oak deeper into the woods. Come fall, I'd hoped to bag a buck with a good-sized rack. The apples would help ensure that.

As the light began to wane overhead, we made out a mound of some kind in the distance next to the path. Further on, we spotted another such mound and speculated what it might be. Almost as soon as we'd spotted the mounds, we smelled an awful stench and I knew then what it was.

"Possums," I said before she could ask. "I ain't never seen traps out here. Looks like somebody's been dumping them."

She covered her nose and mouth with her hands, and I told her not to look. "Who would do such a thing?" she asked.

"Trappers. They take what they want and throw back the rest."

"They don't even eat them?"

"God no. They're terrible eatin.' Unless you're starving. But they could at least take them to the dump."

"The dump? Ain't their lives worth nothing?"

"No. Just their hides," I said. I led her by the hand down the path and stopped at the base of the white oak that held my deer stand. I cut another apple in half and rubbed it over the bark of nearby trees and then poked a small limb through one section of the apple so it would be left hanging low to the ground where deer could reach it. "Them damn possums is liable to draw predators," I said. "Might spook my deer."

"What kind of predators?"

"Cats, most likely. Coyotes maybe."

"Let's go," she said.

"Naw, let's sit a while and watch the stars. We can climb up in the deer stand. It's safe up there," I said. "Ain't nothing going to want us no way with all them possums laying right out like that. Them carcasses ain't putting up no fight, but we will."

I helped her climb the make-do ladder me and my buddies had fashioned by nailing wood slats directly into the tree. We were both glad when we reached the top. I had one apple left and I peeled it and offered it to her, but she made me take some too. I cut off pieces one at a time and we ate it slow, leaning up against the trunk of that big tree. Lightning bugs were just beginning to flicker in the dusk, and little by little we forgot about the possums.

I laid back on the deer stand to look up at the sky, but no stars were out that night. The moon was bright, though, and it lit her face in a pretty white light that made her skin take on the look of a glass doll. It was peculiar how she'd gotten prettier each time I'd seen her, and lying there in the dark beside her my heart began to pound because I knew that she would give herself to me if I asked her to. And I wanted her to something fierce.

"You've done this before, I guess," she said.

"Not many times," I answered back, which was the truth.

"Your friends . . ." She didn't finish.

"Don't worry about them. They're idiots," I said.

"Like you."

I smiled, though I was nervous. "Yeah, like me," I said, ashamed of how I'd treated her.

"You still want Jessica?"

"No," I lied. "She don't know I exist anyhow."

"That's true," she said, and I caught her smiling a little. I kissed her then and pulled my shirt over my head and spread it out on the rough planks where she wouldn't get splinters. The warm night air felt good on my skin, which seemed suddenly drawn tighter over my body. I unbuttoned her denim shorts and shimmied them over her hips.

I was of two minds now whenever I looked upon her. There was the knowledge that what I thought I was seeing was not real. Her stories had filled my mind with impossibilities. Gods sending great scorpions to punish and kill, dogs bearing blazing faces, sisters turned into doves or stars. And then there was also the seeing of my teenage, peckerwood body that peered through the blue blaze of desire. Her skin was soft and took on a fever as I touched her. I had the feeling that something imaginary was happening. I'd heard tell from Uncle Estil and other old timers that witches and wood fairies were known to play pranks on boys in these mountains. If there was tangles in your hair that meant a witch was riding you. But my hair was too short to tangle, and anyway I didn't care if she'd cast a spell on me or not. I'd never felt this peculiar feeling before, and I didn't want it to end.

That's when we heard something creeping up on us, sticks breaking under its weight as whatever it was came to stand at the base of the tree we were messing around in.

"Oh, god. What's that?" she asked, her voice sinking as she spoke.

I held up a hand to shush her while I listened. A deer wouldn't have been so heavy stepping. A cat would've been up that tree already. Unless maybe it was crouching. Still, it didn't feel like a cat. Whatever it was had taken no interest in the possums as I'd guessed. I could feel the heft below us, but it was spread out, not just at the base of our tree but beneath others as well.

I felt groggy, like I'd been drinking, stories swirling around from different times in my life, campfire tales, Indian legends, aliens sightings, all mixing with the stars now, and a cold draft crept up my bare back when I realized something bad was bound to happen. That's the way it always was with stories. Right when you're sucked in is when all hell breaks loose. Everything inside me turned dead as a stump. I wished maybe she were a witch, but with the pull of desire now broke, I knew it had all been fool thinking.

"You think it's coyotes?" she asked.

"Nah," I told her, guessing maybe it was my idiot buddies come fooling. "Ain't nothing," I said.

She started putting her clothes back on, though, and I reached for mine as well.

I saw then that it was the trappers, dumping another tarp load of carcasses. Where in the hell were all these possums coming from, I wondered, but it didn't make no never mind to me. All I knew was this bullshit was spooking away my deer and making a hell of a mess on Uncle Estil's land.

"Hey!" I hollered down from the deer blind, and the girl pulled my shoulder to hush me up and then moved up tight behind me.

A magnum flashlight came swinging around to spotlight us, followed by a couple of roughneck laughs.

"Are you getting you some, young feller?" one of the men asked, and the pair cackled again.

I wished I'd thought to bring my rifle.

The girl couldn't help herself; she had to see what lay in their tarps, and when she leaned forward on her knees to have a look over my shoulder, she caught sight of some of the possums moving. Or at least she thought she did. She cried out, thinking she'd seen one's babies or something. The more upset she got, the louder the trappers laughed at us.

"What's all that hissing up there?" one said. Apparently whatever spell the girl had put on me did not affect them.

"I can see why you brung one as ugly as that out here," the other said, shining his flashlight in both our faces and blinding us with insults. "I hope you brung a rubber. You know them things carry disease, don't you?"

They were having a good time now, but they'd gone too far.

"Shut your damn mouth," I shouted. "Say another word—"

They laughed some more. "Alright there, young buck. Take it easy. Enjoy the rest of your romantic date."

His buddy pulled the tarp from under the carcasses, and the two of them began to make their way back to wherever they came from, talking loudly and joking about the pitiful state of my affair with this old girl. "He's a real catch, too. Ain't he?"

"Yeah. Big spender."

Their voices trailed behind them through the woods until the girl and I were alone again. I felt horrible, worse than I'd ever felt about anything. But I knew the truth too, that I wouldn't talk to the girl again. Probably ever. I wouldn't ever be that man, big enough to share that old girl's burden. I was weak, and I would be all my life, hiding behind prettier women.

The girl was stepping around me now, bawling, making her way down the ladder to find her way home. And I just sat there and watched her go.

Crazy Checks

———

Ira was repairing breaks in his yarn when Charmie started talking about his cousin's girlfriend's kid's crazy checks. "Six hundred dollars a month, him twenty-one year old."

That kind of money got Ira's attention, as it would anybody's. "What's wrong with him?" He tied the yarn at the bobbin level, trimmed the ends with his nippers, and turned the spinning machine back on.

"Not a damn thing," said Charmie. "Healthy as a pig. Goverment ought to ship his sorry ass to North Korea and send all these foreigners with him."

"Nuke their asses," Ira said. Three of his machines were running bad.

"I heard that. Stupid-ass goverment. Here you take some old lady, ain't got money to buy her medicine, and the goverment says they'll give her twelve dollars a month food stamps. Fucked up," Charmie said. He was doffing already, moving down his machines replacing full bobbins with empties, tossing the full bobbins into the wagon. Charmie and Ira were both good doffers, could get all 216 bobbins done in fifteen minutes. But damn if Ira's machines weren't giving him a time.

"Can't grow tobacco no more either," said Ira. "They ain't going to leave us nothing to do." Last night he'd run core yarn and that had kept him from making his hanks. And now this.

"No, but you can make *wi-ine*. I member when this county was dry. Not so long ago neither. And wine, now, that's a hell of a improvement. Ain't seen nobody killed in a car wreck because of cigarettes. Have you?" Charmie came around to Ira's other machine and helped him fix some of his breaks.

"It's the damn Internet. Computers changing everything."

In the break room, Charmie studied the sandwiches in the vending machine. His wife had packed him two pimento cheese sandwiches, but he was still hungry. "Three damn dollars for a week-old sub," he complained. "To hell if it even pays to come to work."

Ira unscrewed the top of his thermos and poured a cup of coffee.

"By the time you figure what gas costs and then your eats and every nickel and dime that gets bled out of you here by Girl Scout cookies and baby showers and bullshit, it don't pay a man to work."

Ira wanted a cigarette with his coffee, but he couldn't have one there. "Going out for a smoke."

"I'll come with you," Charmie said. "Damn shame a man's got to walk clear across the parking lot to stand in the rain and smoke. Smoke-free workplace, my ass. Damn communist goverment."

They walked through the spinning room to the exit and over to Ira's pickup, parked beside the Hardee's dumpsters. Ira was glad it was raining. At least the dumpsters weren't swarming with yellow jackets and reeking of rotten food.

Ira opened the door of his truck and climbed behind the steering wheel. Charmie climbed in the other side and rolled down the window to let the smoke escape. He'd already lit up halfway through the parking lot. Let security say something to him.

Ira reached over and opened the glove box, pulled out a pack of Dorals. He used to smoke Marlboros back when he could afford them. Now Dorals weren't that cheap either. "Seems to me, we're the chumps," Ira said.

"What's that?"

"Chumps. You got twenty-one-year-olds out there know how to pull it over on old farts like us. You think kids like that're ever going to work?"

"Hell no," said Charmie.

"Hell no's right. And whose social security you think that punk's bleeding?"

"Ours."

"Damn straight." Ira took a hard drag on his cigarette, squinted from the smoke curling up into his eyes, and thought to himself how the world was going to hell in a Chinese-made hand basket.

* * *

"All we got to do," Charmie said, "is say our nerves is bothering us."

"Nerves, huh?"

"If you want the crazy check. If you want the disability check, then you got to get hurt here at work."

"Get caught in the spinning frame or something?"

"That'd do it."

Ira studied the spinning machine. It could yank your arm good if you weren't careful. But there was a shutoff button that ran the length of the frame. It would look suspicious if you let the damn machine grab you and never hit the shutoff.

He studied further. Unless it got hold of both your arms, he thought. Then you'd be good and hurt, but not killed or maimed. He didn't want to lose fingers or anything.

Charmie said he was just going to try for his nerves. Said the kid he knew hadn't worked a lick and the government had agreed that the pressures of life were just too much for him. "You believe that shit? Pressures of life."

"What're you going to tell them?" Ira asked, sizing up other potential hazards. There was oil everywhere. The floors were slick as goose shit. He might fall and dislocate his back.

"I'm going to say the economy is scaring me. I'm afraid my job's going to be sent overseas and the strain of all this worrying is making me nervous as a whore in church."

It sounded reasonable to Ira. Maybe the crazy check was the way to go. Probably have to talk to a shrink once a month, though, and they might be trained in ways of seeing through BS and then the check would be cut off and his job would be lost and he'd be screwed. Nah, he thought. Better make it good if you're going to do it.

* * *

Charmie took a nervous fit in the break room, turned over the vending machine with the week-old sandwiches, and all he got was wrote up. "That's alright," he told Ira. "Got to be documented."

A couple days later, he sat on the box all night and watched his machines turn off. When the supervisor came by and told him to get the lead out, Charmie said, "What's the point?" and stared a hole through his head.

"The point is you're going to miss your damn hanks."

"So?"

"What the hell's a matter with you? You miss your hanks, you go home. You go home, you stay home."

Ira was loading spools at the top of his machines. "He'll be alright, Gordon. I'll cover him tonight."

Gordon walked over to Ira's machines. He was an alright guy, Gordon was. Never reported anybody for climbing out the window onto the other building and smoking pot. Not that Ira or Charmie ever did shit like that. But it was alright of him, they thought. He wasn't a fink.

"He's just depressed or something," Ira said. "Disgusted with the futility of living is what he told me."

"Is that right?" Gordon said. "I never knowed old Charmie to be queer like that."

"Me neither," said Ira, taking a look at Charmie sitting on the box, eyes closed, apparently asleep.

Gordon walked over and stood in front of him. Charmie opened his eyes, saw Gordon's black Nikes on the floor, said, "Amen" and jumped to his feet. When he remembered he was suffering from a case of bad nerves, he sat back down on the waste box, reached in and grabbed a handful of yarn, and stuffed it in his mouth.

"Good God," Gordon said. "What the hell." He smacked Charmie's hand and yarn went flying into the frame. "You taking them Mini Thins from the convenience store?"

"No," Charmie said. He didn't know what Mini Thins were, but he figured he ought to find out. "What'd I do?"

"What'd you do? Shit, man, you messing with me?"

"Nah," said Charmie, pretty as you please. "I feel kind of weird."

"You got the actions to prove it," said Gordon.

"You going to document it?" said Charmie.

"What for? All you did was stuff yarn in your mouth."

"I mean not making my hanks." Charmie lowered his eyes but lifted them now and then to get a read on what Gordon might be thinking.

"Not making your hanks is already documented on your hank counter."

"Hmm," said Charmie. "Guess so. So you ain't going to do nothing to me?"

"What is it exactly you want me to do?" Gordon said.

"Nothing," Charmie said quick.

"You're acting peculiar. Everything alright?"

"Suppose I am. Jumpy as a rabbit. All juttery inside. Can't figure what's wrong with me," Charmie said.

"You're like to get a finger jerked off if you get too juttery around these machines," Gordon warned.

"Boy, that's the truth," Charmie said. "You reckon I should go see the nurse about something that'll settle me down some?"

"You ain't going down there to flirt, are you?"

"Lord, no, Gordon. Look at my hands." He held a hand out to prove how shaky feeling he was.

"Alright. But don't you be loving up on Martha down there now." Gordon chuckled. He thought that was real funny.

When Charmie came back, he told Gordon he needed to step out on the roof and smoke a joint with the dopers.

"Say what?"

"That's the only thing here that'll calm my nerves enough so I can work."

"What did the nurse say?"

"She said my blood pressure was sky high, said my heart rate's dangerous."

"And she said you need to go smoke pot?"

"Not in so many words," Charmie said. "Told me to find some St. John's wort, but you tell me how I'm going to find something like that tonight?"

Gordon studied a minute. Charmie's face was bloodless and sweaty. "Alright," he said. "But I don't know nothing, you understand?"

Ira couldn't hear the conversation now. Gordon's voice had dropped below the roar of the machines. He watched Gordon clap Charmie on the arm a couple times and motion for him to shut down two of his frames. Then he walked over to Ira and said, "Watch Charmie's machines for a few minutes there, sport. He's going to step outside and get some fresh air. Ain't feeling too keen."

Ira had no idea what Charmie might do next. No telling. Might jump off the damn roof for all Ira knew. He didn't like getting stuck with his machines either, but he figured if it'd help old Charmie unfold his master plan and get a crazy check, he'd abide it this once.

The thought occurred to him, too, that now might be a good time to get himself caught up in one of the machines. The company might be less suspicious under the circumstances. A man working an extra set of frames, and ordered to do it by a company man. It was just asking too much of any employee, even one as productive and reliable as him, Ira Donald Hutchins, an operator at No. 2 Mill who'd worked fifteen years without incident. If he played his cards right, Ira might get the disability check *and* the crazy check. Losing a job is a demoralizing experience for a man, he tried out saying to himself. Being a cripple would have to be worse.

Charmie's machines were all to hell by now. His own would be, too, by the time he fixed the breaks in Charmie's yarns. He was just about ready to doff his own frames again, and as he loaded new bobbins in the waiting picks, he tried to imagine how he'd do it. It went against human nature to do crazy shit you knew was going to hurt you. And just how bad it would hurt, he couldn't say. Being grabbed by a round steel-beam machine, turning spindles at a velocity of 20,000 rpms was bound to dislocate a shoulder and tear off a fair amount of hide. Oh, he could imagine much worse happening in the warp room or the card room. Getting caught in the carding machine, a big hopper the size of a dumpster, would no doubt kill a man, cut his arm off or crush him, at bare minimum.

Ira thought about the disability check to get his mind off the particulars of the maiming he was about to force upon himself. He and Charmie weren't that old yet, and he didn't mind working. Work had never been a beef for him. And he wasn't that picky. Work was work. He couldn't quite imagine what he'd do with himself after it was all said and done. A man had to fill his days with something. Work was as good a distraction as anything else, he'd found.

Now Charmie, he'd probably like the time off, spend it fishing or hunting or four-wheeling. But Ira didn't much care for things like that. He couldn't really feature in his mind what he'd do, and so he began to question the soundness of the whole undertaking. What was a man's arm worth to him? Six hundred dollars a month? Eight hundred? And how would he scrape by on that? He didn't make much at the mill, but he was clearing double that now. He would have to work under the table to make up the difference, so what would he gain except a busted shoulder?

It was the principle that had bothered him, a generation coming up of moochers, drawing checks, lying around playing video games and getting high.

He lifted the full bobbins into the wagon and pushed it down the line with his hip. The spool hooker had come earlier and picked up his empty spindles, left him new bobbins. He watched the leads of cotton, feeding into the machine, nearly weightless spools of fluff spun down into tight, strong thread. He hated to think what the future looked like. Charmie's frames set waiting for him.

Then a stroke of genius hit him, a thought so good and clear it had to have come from the Almighty Himself, who Ira believed watched over him even though he didn't deserve it. He hadn't been the kind of god to spoil a man, but He had been a good god, one Ira relied on when things got tough, as they were bound to do in a simple man's life. He'd always found that expression funny. The simple man's life was pretty damn complicated, far as he could tell. Yet the complicated man's life looked simple. He didn't mind being called a simple man. He guessed he was what the complicated man thought of as down-homey or some such shit. If the complicated man had that kind of time to sit around pondering about the salt of the earth and all that, seemed like he'd be the one called the simple man.

Any damn way, the Lord seemed somehow to be intervening, giving Ira thoughts he probably wasn't creative enough to come up with on his own, though he prided himself on having a healthy dose of common sense. That's how he figured it must've come from the Lord, 'cause it didn't make a hell of a lot of common sense. It must've been mystical, some kind of divine inspiration like all them poets down at the wine festival talked about.

This was what the Lord said: Charmie's machines ain't been maintenanced properly.

Ira thought for a minute. Was Charmie going to get hurt? Had the Lord already been working in their favor? Or was the Lord telling him to act right now?

He heard a commotion outside where the dopers were loafing around on the roof. "Call 911," somebody hollered inside. "Charmie's fell off the freaking building!"

Ira knew then it was no accident. The Lord had hurled Charmie over the edge of that roof as sure as people in hell want ice water. There was something going on. He felt funny, sort of sparkly inside somehow. Gordon came running into the spinning room, hollering for somebody to get Martha to see if she could tend to Charmie while the ambulance came.

"Shut these damn machines down," Gordon yelled. "I don't want somebody taking a finger off because of all this distraction. OSHA'll be up my ass like ten foot up a bull."

Ira killed his bank of machines and then walked around the frames to Charmie's machines. "I got Charmie's frames, boss," he yelled at Gordon's back. Gordon was standing at the window, trying to get a look at Charmie lying somewhere down in the yard. Talk about a case of bad nerves, Gordon had one. Wait till they found out old Gordon allowed people to hang out on the roof instead of taking their breaks in the break room. Ira felt kind of sorry for him. Gordon ought to jump out the damn window himself, poor bastard.

Hit the kill switch, the Lord said. Ira didn't want to turn Charmie's machines off until he figured out how he was going to get himself hurt. Kill switch, he heard again. It didn't make no sense, but what did Ira know about divine inspiration? He trusted the Lord and hit the kill switch.

At that moment, fire shot through Ira's body. If somebody had dabbed a voltmeter to him, he'd have burned up the needle. He was more than ready to turn loose of the kill switch, but it wouldn't let loose of him. He just stood there conducting electricity like a cheap Taiwan toaster.

If Gordon hadn't turned around and seen him jerking, Ira swore he would've spontaneously combusted in just another second.

"Holy, Jesus!" Gordon yelled. "Somebody hit the main frame!"

* * *

The paper reported both accidents very dramatically alongside another article about the mill sending a hundred machines to El

Salvador. Charmie's urine had revealed a controlled substance in his system, so his insurance refused to pay for the ER visit where he had to have his ankle set. He had only fallen eighteen feet, and because he was high, his body was limber and softened the impact. Gordon was forced to write him up for screwing around on the job. Gordon had had to lie and say he had no idea anybody was hanging out on the roof, and he certainly had no idea they were smoking pot. Nobody ratted him out.

Ira spent a month in the burn center at the Baptist hospital. His fingers were burnt bad. All his fingernails came off. He had all of his fingers, though, thank the Lord. But it wasn't clear how well he'd be able to use them now. The mill sent flowers, probably paid for by money collected in the spinning room, Ira thought.

Charmie came by covered in lint every day after work to check on him, cried like a bawl-baby every time he looked down at poor old Ira's mangled hands. He was feeling guilty for having talked Ira into pulling such a stupid stunt. The accident report couldn't find any reason for Charmie's machines malfunctioning like they did. When they looked back at the maintenance records, though, they discovered several lapses. It was all inconclusive, but there appeared to be no foul play. An act of God, they called it, recommending full restitution for Ira's pain and suffering.

"I guess God knowed what He was doing," Charmie said, sitting on the portable potty in Ira's private hospital room.

Ira stared up at the fluorescent light panels covered in vinyl images of cottony looking clouds, presumably to make one think of heaven, he guessed, although heaven was the last thing on his mind. He was thinking of the last jar of apple butter his wife had put back in the cellar two summers ago. His mother had always cooked up both apples and pears in a big copper pot outside over a fire. But Evelyn had cooked hers in an electric

Crock-Pot and added a packet of Kool-Aid, which he had never heard tell of before.

His thoughts jumped then to tobacco, how carefully his daddy had pulled the little seed plants from the Styrofoam planters and set them out in rows one by one. How together, he and his brothers and sisters had pinched off the heads and the suckers to make the plants grow strong and leafy. Then going back later and spudding each plant onto a stick so it could field-wilt. He was thinking of a little plot of land his daddy often talked about.

It was funny when he looked back over his life, all the crazy shit he'd gotten into out of his own ignorance. He didn't have any damn fingernails. Two of his knuckles on one hand were soldiered together like pipe fittings. They would have to break the bones and reset them.

Charmie reached into his hip pocket and offered Ira a chew of Beech-Nut. He knew the nurses would be all over him if either one of them lit up a cigarette. He wiped at a piece of lint tangled up in his eyelashes. "God's got a plan what we all don't know," he said.

Nympho

Villard Spivey would soon be moving out of middle school and into the halls of Pierce Central. Until then, by authority of his mighty fore knuckle and fickle nature, he ruled my bus like a dithering maniac—casting off his usual stoner poise and suddenly throwing his lanky white arms into wild frog punches that would've given grown men Charley horses. But the most petrifying thing about Villard was the creepy port-wine stain splattered across his chin.

One time a kid said it looked like a chinstrap. Like the ones polo players wore, he said, completely oblivious that the cast-iron knuckles dangling at Villard's side were about to strike with pitiless aim at his bicep.

To the unsuspecting, Villard looked too frail to lay the kind of hurtings on people he did. He was a head taller than any of us, but he moved too slow and smiled too much for people to see what a threat he really posed. You had to have witnessed it before, and we all knew that Villard's bones seemed to have been curiously sharpened like tools under the thin veneer of skin that held them together. And no one could tell when or if he'd strike. Sometimes he took things in stride. It was weird.

But the kid who'd made the chinstrap comment was new, a sixth-grader, and didn't know what a sore spot the birthmark was. Villard struck like a whip while the rest of us waited for their bones to connect, watching with perverse interest for the kid's muscle to hop.

"Next time it's your gonads," Villard warned.

The boy was dumbstruck, although he'd actually giggled afterwards, a high girlish laugh full of fear and gratitude.

On the last day of school, Villard and his friends, a skuzzy-looking kid named Sammy Greene and a commando-wannabe, Wade Roten, were carrying on a hushed conversation and passing a sheet of notebook paper between the seats in front of me. I overheard the word *mattress* and slunk down in my seat. Recently, I'd given people the impression that I knew a girl named Wendy Stuckey better than I actually did. Had she not been the prettiest girl around, and had I not been so credible, Villard and his buds wouldn't have taken such a keen interest in the rumor I'd started.

But the unfortunate fact was that Wendy was my girl. Well, not really, but I wished she were. For the longest time, I'd survived on the idea that if she only knew me, she would be. When that proved not to be true, though, I guess I got a little mad and scratched the words WENDY STUCKEY IS A NYMPHO on the back of a bus seat. Also, I said some things I shouldn't have. Namely, I said she'd lured me into the woods and nailed me on a grungy mattress.

No one doubted a word I said, mostly because I said very few, and also because Wendy had been spotted climbing in and out of my bedroom window the summer before when my cousin Robert ran away from home and came to stay with us. He and Wendy drank Michelob ponies on my bed and listened to my contraband Alice Cooper records.

Ordinarily, my parents would've never allowed me to listen to such devil music, but they thought the records were Robert's and didn't object since they were afraid he'd run away from us, too.

"You guys'll be sorry when you find me on the street taking it up the butt by some fag-ass," Robert liked to threaten.

My dad would draw back his fist like he was going to belt him one for speaking so vulgarly in front of my mom, but she would start crying and run to Robert and throw her arms around him. He needed psychological intervention, she said, which her sister over in Arkansas couldn't afford. Robert stayed with us for two months and saw a shrink once a week until my father finally did belt him for calling him a motherfucker after he'd conned me into helping him hotwire a phone up in my bedroom. It was after my dad found out he'd made 160 dollars' worth of long-distance calls to Aunt Tildy back in Arkansas that Robert had called him a motherfucker and gotten waylaid and sent back home.

But before all that, Wendy had spotted him sitting on our picnic table sulking, while I mowed the grass—a job we were supposed to be doing together, him mowing, me trimming, since I was smaller. Until then all I knew about Wendy Stuckey was that she had quit school as a freshman. Also, she had a pool, which meant she was walking around her yard in a bikini every day when all of us from Timber Grove Middle got off the bus. She was oblivious to our prepubescent catcalls. Half the time it would seem she was asleep in a lawn chair: it was rumored that she roved the woods at night with longhaired emaciated high-school boys, carrying dime bags of pot.

After Robert showed up, though, she waved me over to where she and Ellen Rutherford lay greased up on the redwood deck overlooking her swimming pool. Ellen had a tattoo of a flowering vine sprouting up out of her bikini toward her navel.

She was older than Wendy, eighteen or twenty, and we all suspected she was some kind of sexual guru to our budding nympho.

"Who's that guy staying at your house?" Wendy asked me. "I like his hair." Robert was the only kid any of us had ever seen in person with such long hair. It fell to the middle of his back, longer than Wendy's even. None of our parents went for that hippy stuff, especially mine, since they were in Amway and had an "image" to uphold.

"My cousin Robert," I said, and then, wanting to say more, hoping to say something, anything to impress her, I added, "He's from Arkansas."

"I could tell he wasn't from around here," she said. "Maybe you could introduce me sometime."

I hadn't even introduced myself. I doubted if she knew my name, but I said yes anyway. "Come over sometime," I said, sounding too much like my mother speaking to a new member of the Neighborhood Watch program.

I thought she'd call or something first and then ring the doorbell like anyone else, but instead she came pecking at my bedroom window that same night during one of my parents' stupid Amway meetings. Robert wasn't even home and I was in the other room. I'd just found an issue of *Razzle* in my father's nightstand while I was looking for a pair of black socks. They insisted that I ditch my unlaced high tops and flame-bleached jeans for Hush Puppies and cords whenever anyone from the "group" was over. My parents were working toward the diamond level, naively expecting to become millionaires before I started college. They strictly forbade the use of competitor products and stripped our house, throwing away full tubes of Crest, unopened bars of Irish Spring and boxes of Tide, replacing them with plainly packaged goods like Glister, Body Series 4-in-1 and a detergent called SA8 that broke me out in hives.

The magazine had been earmarked in several places, so I'd
flipped there first. One page was a collage of pictures of the
same girl: Amanda, a blond posing in various bits and pieces
of athletic equipment. In one she wore nothing but a goalie
mask and in another only a jockstrap and a whistle with a
football tucked under her left arm. It wasn't the first time I'd
leafed through the magazine, studying and comparing nipple
radiuses, but I still got a boner. And this time Amanda's face
turned into Wendy's. I saw that gum-smacking, trash-talking
mouth, that headband dangling with beads and roach clips,
the necklace with a tiny silver cross resting in the dip of her
windpipe.

Coincidentally, I'd lost my Magic 8 Ball earlier and found
it in my parents' room. Who knows why it was there. Maybe it
was secretly the trusted oracle my parents relied on to make all
their Amway decisions. Or maybe I just forgot it there during
a previous sock and *Razzle* raid. I asked the Magic 8 Ball if this
was really the kind of girl Wendy was, because despite what
everyone said, part of me didn't believe it. Or didn't want to
believe it.

I thought of Wendy's silhouette dancing against the drawn
shade of her window three houses behind mine and to the
left. On Saturday afternoons I'd been able to nearly make out
the faces of the *Tiger Beat* hunks decking her walls. Her room
looked like anyone else's her age or mine. There was something
completely normal about Wendy, and I loved whatever it was.

Looking down at the ball, I asked as formally and completely
as I could (to avoid confusing the ball), "Is Wendy Stuckey
truly to God a nympho?" The answer: "Concentrate and ask
again." I shook the ball again. "Better not tell you now," it said.
"Try again later." Annoyed and losing my boner, I chucked it
into my parents' bed and focused on my glorious erection and
Wendy's face. I saw her bare feet slapping the buckling tongue-

and-groove floor of Carter's Qwik Pick on a day I'd come nearer to touching her than I ever had before. I'd pretended to look for a Whatchamacallit while she got in line behind a grimy old guy buying a newspaper and two tall Buds.

She'd worn cutoffs and a green halter that day, and I hustled in line behind her, inched up as close as possible. I studied a razor knick in the bend of her knee. Noticed that the backs of her arms were a tad bumpy. Admired the way her dark hair feathered into a V, barely striking the knot of her blouse. She'd smelled sweet, but I didn't know what like. I watched her hand the cashier a five and then leave.

I looked out my parents' bedroom window but couldn't see the dripping air conditioner I'd grown so fond of jutting out from Wendy's house. All I saw were cars lining the road in front of my own house and Amway stooges strolling up in their red ties, their pleated wool skirts and corduroy blazers. I knew I had to lose the erection soon but didn't dare touch it. Instead, I shoved the magazine back into my father's sock drawer and snatched up a pair of his ribbed nylon jobs. Then I pulled off my own sweaty rolled-down tube socks and shoved them in his nightstand under the magazine.

As I finished making myself presentable to my parents' underlings, I heard the rapping on my window across the hall. I still had a hard-on the size of Rhode Island when I opened the window and found Wendy standing on my own air conditioner, which lay on the ground next to our house. It had gone on the blink and when my impatient father had failed to fix it, he shoved it out the window and left it there.

"Hey," I whispered, stooping a little for cover. "Why didn't you come to the door?"

She shrugged. "Is Robert home?"

"No," I said. In my anxiety to make her leave but come back later, I'd actually blurted out the answer, and now I worried she wouldn't return because I'd barked at her. I tried again, this time softer. "I mean he's gone now but he'll be back." I smiled, something I hadn't done in the four months since I'd gotten braces. "You want to come back at eight?"

"Okay," she said, whispering now too. Our faces were so close I could almost taste her Dentyne. I still didn't think she knew my name but at least she'd known which window was mine. I'd gotten the crazy notion she'd been watching me all along.

* * *

Villard and his gang got the idea that I should show them where the mattress was. They wanted me to draw a map; they were planning a trip.

I stared at the graffiti splotching the seat in front of me, the same words I'd ignorantly scratched into the bus seat a few months earlier and occasionally considered marking out but was afraid to: WENDY STUCKEY IS A NYMPHO. Words I had then verified with my Magic 8 Ball. "You may rely on it," it said. "Signs point to yes." But now I wasn't so sure, and here was Villard smiling, looking stoned, and wanting proof. I slid my knees up over the graffiti. "I made it all up," I confessed. "There is no mattress. I just wanted—"

Villard clamped his hand down hard over my mouth. "You're lying, man," he said. His pupils were the size of nickels. "Don't you go spreading that shit now, Clayton." His Adam's apple surfaced like a turtle as he moved in on me with his plum-red chin. I smelled the cinnamon toothpick in his mouth and pictured my nuts shattering like sugar cubes from the force of that knuckle, so I moved my health book from the seat to my lap. "There is so a mattress," he said, "and you're going to show us where it's at. You're the only one who knows."

But I didn't know. What did he want me to do?

He stepped on the toe of my shoe. Then, as the bus approached our stop, he and his friends surrounded me and ushered me off. The four of us strolled by Wendy's house together then and Villard informed me that I was going to say something.

"Like what?" I sneered.

"Like I don't give a shit—but it better be good."

I thought I was going to get belted any minute, and I sure as hell didn't want it to happen in front of Wendy, but I couldn't think of anything to yell at her. She hadn't come around since Robert had left, but I didn't think it had anything to do with the rumor I'd started. I figured she'd heard about it, but I didn't think she would've believed that I'd been the one who'd said it. I hoped she wouldn't anyway, especially now that I was sorry. Either way, I didn't expect her to be mad at me. I figured she was probably immune to all of us by now. Villard was rubbing his knuckles in the side of my neck, egging me on.

Someone's dog crossed the road in front of us, urinating on hedges and mailbox posts. It blocked my line of vision, but as we drew nearer, I saw the Coppertone mountains of Wendy's chest. Two little summits outdoing the panorama of the surrounding Carolina foothills. Little patches of bikini topping them like snow crests. I was dying to say something vulgar—so much was off limits to me—but I was equally disgusted with myself, too, now that I'd gotten to know her a little. Finally, I just let out a long ear-piercing whistle, which I'd secretly been practicing for some similar occasion, though I didn't know what exactly. I'd tried out different ways of placing my fingers, attempting two-handed pinkie styles and then later one-handed techniques until by now I could produce hard earsplitting warbles, completely fingerless if I wanted. I liked having a skill Villard and the others envied. I felt a little giddy and a little scared, too. I didn't know what they wanted exactly. I thought of Boyd

Keen, the "Mattress Keen," his local UHF commercial, showing
a warehouse full of bed frames and mattresses and waterbeds. I
didn't get the whole Mattress Keen thing, even though he wore
a crown and carried around a scepter in the stupid ads.

After the whistle, I smiled nervously and gave a little wave
to identify myself. But Wendy lay motionless belly down on a
floatie in the pool. My love song had fallen on deaf ears. She
didn't so much as rearrange her slippery legs. For a minute I
thought she really was ticked at me.

Then, as if on cue, she rose up on both elbows, removed
her mirrored sunglasses from eyes rimmed in metallic-blue eye
shadow about the same color as my father's Monte Carlo, and
executed the most beautiful flip off I'd ever seen. I marveled at
the symmetry of her fingers, the precision of her wrist, snapping
and then thrusting the bird up into the air, higher and higher,
the altitude of her feigned animosity for us penetrating the
heavens.

All around me came a rumbling hoot and then Villard
clapped me on the shoulder. "Fucking A, man! Fucking A!"

* * *

At the Amway meeting that night my mother showed marketing
plans to a group gathered round our kitchen table. "Gilbert
and I used to be like you," she said. "We had the same debts,
the same worries that come with the imprisonment of a *j-o-b*."
The women looked around my mother's kitchen, taking in the
same mismatched appliances they probably had in their own
houses.

A woman with bobby pins in her hair looked incredulously
at my mother. "We're supposed to just quit our jobs?"

"All I'm saying is you have to be *core*," Mom said.

In the den, my father was clarifying some of the
misconceptions of amassing wealth. "Financial freedom is not

a sin; it's God's *reward* for getting your priorities straight,"
he explained. He glanced up at me when I entered the room.
Men and women sat in rows of metal fold-up chairs Mom and
Dad bought specifically for these meetings. I crossed the room
behind them and climbed over the back of our catty-cornered
loveseat.

"What are you looking for, Son?" Dad said. I hated how he
called me *Son* by way of introduction in front of people.

"Nothing." I kicked my feet and turned myself upright.

Dad glared, assuring me I was in for a talking to later.
"Razzle-dazzle 'em," I said then in my mock-motivated voice. I
made a fake jump shot in the air, for good measure. He flexed
the fingers on both hands, straightened his tie, and resumed his
spiel.

* * *

This was Villard's plan: we'd spread the word that I was leading
an expedition (sworn to secrecy) to the spot where Wendy had
banged me and bring back some kind of proof that the mattress
truly existed. It was okay, Villard said, that there actually was no
mattress—we'd come up with one ourselves. More specifically,
I would come up with one—my own. I was to pretend I'd had a
little accident, so my parents would toss my mattress out. And
Villard was spending the night with me to make sure I followed
through. "My parents'll never believe I pissed the bed, you
guys, come on. I'm thirteen," I said. I'd never said the word piss
before, and it gave me a sudden burst of courage.

Then Villard came back with, "They'll believe it when they
see it, mama's boy." Just the mention of my mother made me
guess she probably had some kind of miracle product to clean it
with anyway. She would try the entire product line if necessary
and then take it out of my allowance. I was beginning not to
care how much pain Villard could inflict on me, only I knew it

didn't have to be a one-time thing. He could kick the shit out of me every day until he went away to high school. I wished I'd never said anything, and I couldn't remember now why I had. After all, Wendy and I had kissed.

Let me back up some.

She'd been coming over almost every night to see Robert. They seemed like soul mates for each other, what with Robert's head case and her own sullied reputation. And make no mistake: it was a reputation she'd earned, I was sure, since she and Robert got it on that first night—right in front of me.

I didn't complain any; it was way better than *Razzle*, and it wasn't like I actually knew Wendy enough to seriously doubt the things people said about her. Sure, in my mind I made her wholesome and misunderstood, but when she was there in front of me, shining my cousin's knob, I mean what else could I think? In a way there really was a mattress, and it really was mine.

But there was something faithful about her, too. She came by regularly, and I was sure she was only seeing us. She knew Robert wouldn't be staying forever, and sometimes I got the idea that she was really doing me—vicariously, of course, but still, me. I thought she knew that if she actually touched me, I'd go up like a roman candle. Burst into flames. Something. I needed the distance, a buffer zone. I was still too young.

The kiss, though, was different. Wendy wasn't the most tactful person I'd ever met, but she was sensitive. That particular day she'd studied me while we listened to records and waited for Robert to return from his shrink's. I could tell she wanted to ask me something, and she could see it made me nervous. I knew it had something to do with my virginity and knew too that if she spoke of it, I would loathe seeing her ever again and quite possibly run away from home as Robert had. Finally, she decided not to say anything; she just leaned over and brushed her lips against mine, and I froze with terror. I had just caked a bunch of wax on my braces and didn't want to gross her out. The door to my room swung open then and I jumped up and ran around behind Robert and down the hall to the bathroom. She'd only giggled a little, but it shot down the hall to my ears like birds squawking as they settled into a tree.

* * *

When Villard showed up that afternoon with his duffle bag, ready to spend the night, my parents got a little concerned. My mother checked in on us frequently, as if she expected to find me hung by the neck from my bunk bed with the curtains to my room flapping in the wind and Villard vanished into the night. Frankly, I worried about this too, but later, when Villard had gone to the bathroom, I told her he was spending the night so I could experiment on his birthmark. "I told him you might have something to clear it up," I said.

It had been an easier sell to Villard than I expected. I shuddered to think that I'd wind up selling Amway one day myself. But where my nuts were concerned, I was motivated.

"So I got this stuff," I said on the bus. I stacked a book in my lap.

"What kind of stuff?"

"Stuff for your ah . . . A kind of ointment for ah . . . the . . ."

"My strawberry?" Villard raised his eyebrows, tilted his head.

"Yeah," I said, bracing myself. "It's my parents, you know. They sell this shit that's supposed to be good for everything. All we have to do is mention it, and they'll let us do whatever we want."

"Well, what is it? Will it lighten it?" he asked, unexpectedly hopeful sounding.

"Maybe," I said. "My dad uses it to scrub tar off fender wells."

"I thought you said it's an ointment."

"I said it was a *kind* of ointment." I paused, worried I might've struck the wrong key, but Villard was still listening. "My mom thinks it's some kind of miracle. She puts it on sunburns, bug bites, scratches. Stuff like that."

"It ain't aloe vera, is it? I tried aloe vera—that don't do jack."

"Nah. This is stuff they sell, called L.O.C.," I said.

"L.O.C.? What's it mean?"

"I don't know. Who cares? It's just a cover, man. Shit."

"Okay, settle your horses, hoss."

It was still a dumb plan, but I'd just have to think on my feet. I hadn't actually intended on experimenting with my parents' Amway products, but as soon as Villard arrived he wanted to get started.

"Where's the ointment?"

I sighed. "Hang on." He followed me into the laundry room where I dug around in cabinets for the jug of L.O.C. It was almost empty. "Here," I said. "All you need's a dab."

Villard uncapped the plastic bottle and turned it upside down over his hand, but nothing came out.

"Shake it," I suggested.

"It's empty, man," Villard said. "Shit. Look for some more. Your parents sell this stuff, right? They gotta have an inventory somewhere."

I didn't exactly feel like playing doctor with a psychopath like Villard, but I also didn't want to piss my mattress, so I guessed I might as well be grateful for the diversion.

"Let's look in the garage. My dad—"

"Yeah," Villard said. "The bumpers." He looked skeptical, the way he had on the bus, but he was still willing to give it a look. "I never heard of no shit that would clean a bumper and take care of your zits, too."

"I know. It's weird," I said. "Just come on."

As we were making our way to the garage, the doorbell rang. "Mom!" I yelled through the house. It rang a second time. "M-*o-o-o-o-m-m*!" I tried again. But it rang a third time, so I had to answer it, and when I did, there was Wendy Stuckey.

"Hey," she said by way of hello. "You said to use the door."

Villard came up behind me from the garage with a stripe of beige paste smeared over his birthmark. I had no idea what he'd found and put on himself, and I didn't care. He was as surprised to see Wendy as I was, and he wiped his face with the neck of his shirt as fast as he could, but Wendy had already spotted something on his chin.

"You boys doing each other's makeup?"

Villard laughed nervously. "Haha. Good one, Wendy."

God, he was worse than I was. I rolled my eyes, and Wendy laughed a little.

"Anyway," she said, reaching up to unfasten a feathered roach clip from her hair. "I just wanted to give you this as a way of saying thank you for starting a vicious lie about me! Little turd!" She threw the roach clip at me and shot me the finger as she walked back down the sidewalk in front of our house. My soul burst into about a million flames.

"Fucking A!" said Villard. "That was too easy. Wendy Stuckey just waltzes up and hands us proof! Fucking A!"

"Shhhh! Shut up. My mom'll hear you, man! Shit."

"Sorry," he said, then mouthed the stupid words silently. Fucking A!

"No," I said. I was sick of Villard's crap. I was tired of being terrorized. "No, fucking A!" I said, at the top of my voice. I didn't care if my mom heard me or not.

There were still a few lingering streaks of whatever Amway product he'd smeared on his face, and I hoped it would leave an oozing rash worse than the port-wine stain he was so self-conscious about. I wanted to punch something . . . him! I wanted to beat the living shit out of him, even though I knew he'd pulverize me. Reflexively, I bent my fingers on both hands, all my fear and frustration and sorrow about what I'd done to Wendy calcifying in the bony ridges of my knuckles. All it would take now was a fast tap, a lightning bolt right to the forehead maybe. Or no, maybe right in the pec muscle where it'd ache for days and leave a monster bruise. I mean, this douchebag fully expected me to piss my own bed! Ha! And I was going along with it! Double douchebag!

"Arggghhhh!" I yelled, and Villard cowered a little and looked at me nervously.

"Settle your horses, hoss."

And that was it. I wound my arm back and pecked him hard as I could right between the eyes. Pain shot through my own hand and up my elbow. It felt like I'd broken my finger. I probably had. My mother would have to take me to the emergency room to have a splint put on. But I didn't care.

A knot swelled up on Villard's forehead the size of an eyeball. He cursed and rubbed it a minute, but then he struck me hard, before I could even see it coming, right in the nads. I doubled over and puked. "Fucking A!" I said.

This Low Land of Sorrow

He could hear the children playing under the apple trees. The bare limbs would be bearing buds red as a mother's nipple. Snakes underfoot keeping watch on their hard labor, the found cinder blocks and planks laid out straight, the pretending walls of their little houses.

The cellar door lay just under his bed, and he could feel it flung open, the sunlight licking between the apple trees, dappling its damp stairs where company descended unchaperoned to sample his wife's shelves of pickled corn and chow-chow, her okra and succotash. Sooner or later they would edge up to his bed, cradling jarred beans in the crooks of their elbows and patting his veiny hand, while the children's mother, his wife's daughter-in-law, spoke softly to him.

"Bill, it's Cecil come to see you." "It's Wendell." "It's Brother Mullins from Little Dove." "It's Janice." "Mabel."

Down through the branches and the limbs and the boughs where all the cradles lay rocking. All the babies and the babies' babies. Half-remembered voices and the ghost-torches of silhouettes bending near his blind eyes.

In the next room there was preaching. Hard preaching, which he'd never cottoned to. The word Jezebel flew around the house and landed like a mortar shell in the room where he lay, the young daughter-in-law its obvious target, a dress too short for passing through to heaven, suited more for this low land of sorrow. The words hot but her hands cool against his abdomen, bandaging, and his hands now, floating unsteady in the air, signing his name to the parcel of bottomland he meant for her to have. Had he not warned the girl and her husband, too? Too late now. He was not long for this world.

He heard water running in the pipes of the new bathroom and wondered whether the children had come in. He hoped they had. They liked the toilet flusher about as much as they liked to push the knob on the television when he said they could. They were good children, not nearly mischievous enough, though he had sometimes felt the boy standing before him, face to face as he rested in the recliner and listened to the news. He could hear them whispering to their mother about cartoons, her shooing them back outside to play. But the boy would sneak back and stare in his face. He had felt his milky breath fog the lenses of his useless spectacles, the boy standing bright as a torch before him, a wildness building in him the longer he waited until at last he ran outdoors and sent all his grandmother's cement chickens and ducks, rolling down, down the hillside, all but the big rooster upon which he'd climb astride as if in a saddle.

This news all gathered later from their mother's scolding. "You put every one back where it came from," she'd demand.

And the old man could see it then, the yard ornaments toppling down the steep embankment, their heavy imprints in the grass, standing empty as an egg carton.

The bottom was the first piece of property he'd owned as a young man. A small parcel, just two acres, but lush and flat. Good pasture for horses. He'd fenced it, built a small barn, room for hay and two stables, one for the speckled mare he rode and another in case he acquired a gelding. He was a sawyer at the mill, but he'd told his mother his designs. Timber. The next parcel would have stands of healthy hardwood. He'd known before most that chestnut was no good, the burls and knots touted to buyers as part of its characteristic beauty, what made it one of a kind. But he'd steered clear of the blight, invested in hickory, oak, hemlock, locust. Locust made good fence post. Nothing fancy. Only what folks needed.

* * *

He'd sent for the woman after his first wife had died, all the children moved off. She'd come to stay with people she knew, renters in the little cinder-block house he owned down the way. He'd seen her come and go, three little boys at the hem of her skirt. In a hard way, needing charity but disinclined to ask. Forty years old? Maybe younger. None too attractive, but his sight was failing him anyway. He'd sent and she'd come, and now all this belonged to her.

"*Jezebel!*" he hears, and his hands fly away, signing the papers, signing the papers. Where was the banker? He'd come yet, like all the rest, and then maybe. Maybe then.

In heaven, there would be a corner for him. So they said. He hoped it was covered in chestnut. He'd walk it off, meets and bounds, stobbing the lines. His eyes would be right again, too, if what they said had any truth. He'd feel the burs underfoot and looking down see the fallen fruit up to the ankle of his boot. He'd look out, surveying the hills and valleys. Maybe another speckled mare. Maybe tobacco. Maybe tomorrow he'd start again.

Justice Boys

———

Rita takes the baby, still screaming, from the tub of water. Lays him on his back on the floor between her legs. Kneads his stomach, fit to burst, with her fingers. Beside them, shards of soap, homemade suppositories. His face the color of cranberries, tonsils raging. He stiffens, bucks when she tries lifting his legs. She is forced to pry him open like a frozen chicken, and even then, the soap does no good, brings neither of them relief.

"Stand away from the windows," she tells the girls, but won't let them leave the room. They want to watch *The Wonderful World of Disney*, but Rita has lit the front room only as much as she has to. "Rock your babies," she says. "They're sleepy."

"Mine has a bellyache," the younger one says, asking for a piece of soap, going to work on the doll when Rita says it's okay, anything to keep quiet. Jenny, the eldest, doesn't offer to take up her own doll. She pulls her sister to the floor covered in Cheerios, bribes her with toy bottles of orange juice. She turns the bottle up to the doll's mouth, watches the fluid inside disappear.

"Not orange juice," the littler one says. "Castor oil." Her brother's cries do not faze her like they do her mother.

The baby, five weeks old, lies down hard on his scream, though now his throat tightens in a hushed blue choke that scares Rita more than the locked bowels, more than the Justice boys outside.

Arjay is still gone with Cleanth, but the Duster's in the yard, and that's what draws them, firing their shots now and again at the bag of dog food leaning next to the house or at the tulip-shaped retreads Arjay cut up to hem in the peonies.

They leave the car alone, useless to her as the soap. Useless as Arjay, gone again as always, sometimes three and four days. This time, he took Cleanth and Jimbo and a stick of dynamite Cleanth swiped from Litwar. Cleanth is half senseless, especially when he's drinking, and that's always. Cleanth told Arjay they were going to finish this thing tonight, but a lot of good that does Rita now, with the Justice boys outside. Hurt, the Justice boy Arjay took a pool stick to at Omie's tavern, is making turkey calls. Rita got a good look at him at Easter, up at the park, when they came driving by slow and pulled their van over by the slides where they could watch the kids.

Hurt's dull eyes followed the children running across the grass, jostling pink and green baskets too big for some. He'd singled out Rita's girls tripping in the hems of their long dresses, the littler one squatting down in a frustrated heap, crying. He knew Rita saw him watching, knew Arjay was watching, too. He'd stuck a gray, leathered arm scabbed over with newly needled tattoos out the window of the van and pointed out Jenny and Sis to his kin with him inside the van.

Arjay had glared at Hurt and turned back to Cleanth and Jimbo and the rest, all fisted up in a huddle, drawing hard on their cigarettes, issuing silent death threats over their shoulders.

Hurt had got a good look at Rita, too, she was sure, wearing polyester pants and sitting on top a picnic table smoking a Kool.

When she saw Hurt, she scraped off the fire against the edge of the cement table and lay the butt down for later. Half in shadow, his arm draping the side of the van, Hurt had smiled, rubbed his hand on the door panel like it might have been Rita's ass and let go a lunatic laugh out the opened black window of the van to where she sat, crossing her arms, hunching forward. The wind had been chapping the kids' cheeks and fingers all morning, but she'd left them alone. Hurt leaned out the window, into the full sun, made a peace sign, then laid his fingers over his mouth and tongued the V that represented Rita.

She gave him the finger, and then Hurt laid down on the horn that issued forth a tinny version of reveille and the kids stopped searching for the lucky egg and looked, panic-stricken, toward the van at the edge of the woods. Hurt gunned the engine and balled tire marks over the pavement. "We're watching!" he called out, and the panel doors swung open wide now to show their number. Rita knew it wasn't even half of them, but still it must've been six, seven maybe.

Wendell, the youngest, had stood behind Hurt's seat, his bare, muscled arms fixed overhead, braced against the van's ceiling to keep from being thrown. His jaw was set and showed the same worry Rita felt. After a minute or two of being taunted by the other men inside the van, he was coaxed into throwing glass bottles against the road as they'd been doing, but Rita sensed that Wendell had values prevailing over the bonds of kinship. He shared the hollowed face of his relatives, the same sharp nose, same deep-set eyes. But the flesh on his back was clean, like his dark, shaggy hair and the whites of his eyes.

Arjay and Cleanth and Jimbo and the others had gone back to their vehicles and stood like sentinels around the perimeter of the park. Hurt stopped the van suddenly in front of Rita and swung an arm out the window, his filthy fingers nearly touching her blouse. She jerked away, but still they were close enough now to pull her into the opened door of the van if they had wanted.

Rita's eyes searched for Wendell, but he'd been slung deeper into the group toward the rear of the vehicle. The others stood in his place, each of them with their eyes locked on Rita's body, some gesturing blowjobs or fondling themselves to put the fear in her. They knew better than to do anything though. There were more guns in that park than at Appomattox.

Inside the house now, Rita almost wishes they'd come in and see for themselves that Arjay's not there. But not really.

The baby has squalled himself into a stupor. He has Arjay's light hair, broad forehead. Rita imagines him full grown, under a carbide light like the one her daddy wore. She can still smell it, still see the buckets of water he carried with him.

Arjay's own wet-cell battery and hard hat hang permanently on a peg by the door with his miner's belt. She'd nearly cried when she washed up his dinner bucket and put it away.

Wildcat strikes have shut down the mines, and this time, Arjay told Rita, he hopes they stick it to the coal bosses good. Carter can order them back in under Taft-Hartley all he wants, he says, but he'll not scab work. Not even if their food stamps are taken. Not even if he's left hunting scrap iron for the rest of his born days.

That's what started things with the Justice boys. Arjay and Jimbo had been driving up and down hollers looking for pieces of scrap iron to sell to Luther Linny over in Mile Branch. Arjay said they drove deep into Mingo County, found themselves in nameless backwoods. Drove clear up the top of a mountain. Was about dark by the time they found anything worth salvaging, an old engine block they threw into the trunk and counted as the day's last.

Arjay says he backed the Duster up onto the bank and turned around. They hadn't seen house lights before then, but all of a sudden, a truck drew up front of them and about twenty big hosses jumped down off its fenders and started cussing Arjay and Jimbo. One took a crowbar and ripped the chrome off the Duster and then smacked Arjay down across the head with his fist. Then the one that hit him walked around and pried the trunk open, said, "This don't belong to you," and rolled the scrap iron down into the branch where it could keep on rusting.

When Cleanth heard what happened, he said, "Let's go kill them son of a bitches," and handed Arjay a stick of dynamite he took off the job. They'd been standing around outside Omie's, a tavern Cleanth laid up at most of the time. Arjay stood listening to Jimbo retell how the nameless elder Justice had cold-cocked him.

"Yeah," Arjay said, "but you get one of them pussies alone."

Hurt had pulled into the gravel lot then and walked brazenly into the beer joint. Arjay had followed Hurt inside and shoved him into a bank of empty stools lining the bar.

"Who the hell!" Hurt yelled, grabbing a pool stick. Cleanth and Jimbo dragged Hurt back toward the pool tables, away from the other drunks, then walked back and sat at the bar and watched the beating Arjay gave Hurt with the pool stick they'd taken away from him.

When Arjay was satisfied Hurt wasn't getting up again, they lit out of the bar, swaggering. Outside, Cleanth reached through the window of the Super Bee and pulled the dynamite out of the glove box, handed it to Arjay. Arjay turned the explosive over in his hand and nodded. "Awright," Cleanth said, and the three of them hopped in the car and took off.

But for all Rita knows, Arjay and Cleanth and Jimbo could be dead, floating somewhere along Tug River. In a few days, they might wash up like those do who meet up with the Justices.

Right now all she really cares about is working the knots out of her infant son's belly. He writhes and screams a white-hot holler and Rita sees the face of her younger brother, dying in a jungle in some place called Lang Vei and realizes there is no getting out of this struggle but by death. The baby sweats and bays low now like something wild from that jungle or from this one, like maybe a mountain screamer. But he quits moving, just like Arminta's baby had, and Rita knows her son has little fight left in him. She grabs him up quick.

"What's wrong, Mommy?" her eldest daughter asks with an aged little face.

Rita surveys the room, finds the keys to the Duster hanging on the nail by the door.

"Nothing, baby," she says. "Everything's awright." But as she cradles the burning hot infant in her arms, Rita tries to remember when she heard the last shot fired at the porch and can't. "We're taking Brother to the clinic." She hopes a doctor will still see her, now that the medical card is gone, but she has to try. "Stay close to me," she tells the girls. "When I open the door, y'all climb in the backseat from this side. Okay? This side closest the house."

"You know how to drive, Mommy?" the littler one asks. "I never seen you drive before. Where's Daddy?"

"Don't be scared," the eldest says, taking her sister by the hand. "Mommy's a good driver. We go driving all the time. Don't we, Mommy?"

"That's right, angel. Now you girls stay behind Mommy and keep quiet as mouses."

"I can keep quieter than a baby mouse this little," says the youngest, measuring a size almost imperceptible with her tiny fingers.

Rita considers turning off all the lights, but decides against it, thinking it better not to do anything that might signal the Justice boys. The baby is quiet now, but she is not grateful and half hopes that when the wind hits him, he'll come screaming back to life. Only the girls wince, though, when the wind lifts the tails of their nightgowns.

"Okay, hurry, hurry, hurry," whispers Rita, holding open the car door. Then she scooches across the front seat and lays the baby beside her. Holding a hand to his hard belly, she fumbles with the keys, but the car won't crank. It hops forward, though, and now she is sure the Justice boys are watching.

They probably saw her all along. Rita imagines one poking another in the ribs when she came creeping outside with the kids. "Lookey, lookey," he probably said, digging an old clump of chew from his jowls and packing in new. She hears another birdcall, turkey or duck or some such, and thinks it sounds like Hurt maybe.

The clinic is in Welch, thirty miles away, but if she can get through the gears, Rita knows she can steer that car all night long if she has to. It is the pedals that bother her. Arjay said to use only one foot for the brake and the gas, but she can't work the clutch to keep the car idling.

"Jen, climb up here and keep a hand on Brother for Mommy."

"I want to," the younger one whines.

"Awright," Rita says. "He can ride between you, but don't be poking him, Sis. He don't feel good."

"I know, Mommy. That's why we're going to the doctor."

"That's right. Now don't hold his belly too tight. Just keep him from falling in the floor." Rita looks at her eldest and then out the back windshield into the dark. She tries again to crank the car, talks herself through it once and then somehow they lurch forward.

Behind her a set of headlights come on and she realizes hers are not. "Shit," she says, twisting knobs until she finds them. She grips the steering wheel with both hands and glances too often in the rearview mirror.

But let them follow her if they want to. They only mean to scare her. She spoke to Wendell once, at the produce stand, when his mother had died. "Real sorry about your mommy," she had offered.

"Thank you, lady," he'd said, and Rita had wondered if anyone had ever called her lady before.

No, she thinks. Wendell won't let the others do anything to her, if he can help it.

But he's the youngest, and Hurt has a score to settle.

"Sing 'the stars at night,' Mommy," the youngest girl says from the backseat.

Rita steps on the clutch and grinds the last gear. The curves scare her, so she touches the brake and the car chugs. "Downshift," she hears Arjay telling her. The car begins to stall, but she pushes the clutch and brings it back to life at a speed she can handle, though the sudden jerking makes the younger girl shriek. "E-e-e-e! Are we wrecking, Mommy?"

"No, Sis," the eldest says. "Mommy's only playing. Right, Mommy?"

Rita's voice is thin as she begins to sing. "The stars at night."

The littler girl belts out the only line she knows. "Deep in the heart of Texas!"

In the dark, Rita can't spot a single star for the heavy swag of tree branches that flank the road as it winds itself around the mountain. The night air is nippy, but she leaves a window down for the baby when what the baby really needs, she knows, is more than a breath of fresh air. Maybe she leaves it down for herself, to cool her face, flushed with heat and worry. The baby hasn't stirred at all, and she doesn't ask if he's alright, just begs God again that he will be.

Behind her, the Justice boys keep a watchful distance, and in Rita's mind they are biding time until she turns the car over the hillside of her own doing. The roads are bad to break off at the edges where coal trucks have softened the asphalt, so she keeps an eye out for potholes that will stall the car and scare the kids and then do in her nerves altogether. The window is fogged from the inside with old cigarette smoke, and the more she wipes at it with her sleeve, the more blurry things outside become. If an animal leaps out, she has already decided she will run it over. Anything to keep from stalling.

"Blow the horn loud, Mommy, when we get to the underpass," Sis says.

"You don't have to honk at night," Jenny says. "You can see the headlights coming."

"I don't care. Will you honk anyway, Mommy? Ple-e-ease?"

"Okay," Rita says. "Now, sit back."

When the road finally straightens out a spell, it comes down along the Tug. Even tinged with mud, and even in the shadows of night, water sparkles now and again like flecks of fool's gold across the wide gulch that is the river's bed. How many fools are down there Rita does not know, but she guesses that Arjay and Cleanth with their dynamite might be. Even if they had already called the other Justice boys out and held the dynamite overhead and said, "Let this be the end of it here and now," that doesn't do Rita an ounce of good. Four or maybe five men are in the vehicle behind her, she is sure, and even with Wendell among them, she has the clearest notion that she and her babies are soon to become a message to Arjay and Cleanth.

On the straightaway, Hurt guns his engine as if he intends to ram Rita from behind. Then he swerves into the passing lane and edges up alongside the Duster. He leans across the seat and two other men and waves fiercely for her to pull over.

Rita trains her eyes on the road, only half glancing at him, and when she does, she sees the van fall back and take up again in the lane behind her. Hurt flashes his lights, swerves the van side to side, playing with her, and she snatches the chance to outrun him. If he reaches the underpass before she does, there is no getting by.

She checks the rearview and suddenly cannot find them. She looks beside her. Nothing. They're in her blind spot, she thinks, and probably gaining on her. She imagines what Hurt will do if he has the chance. She sees his tattooed arms reaching for her, tearing at her clothes.

There is a crack, suddenly, like dynamite, and her head jerks up to look in the mirror just as a tree comes down behind her. If the car had been sitting still, they would have felt its vibration as the tree struck the ground. For half a second, Rita thinks it's Arjay. She looks for him to come sauntering out of the woods with a chain saw in his hand, an invisible circle of firepower around him.

But it's the week of Halloween, and it's only pranksters lighting fires and blocking the road. She and Arjay had done the same kinds of thing when they were kids. At least, she had been party to it, doing her own share of sneaking beers, raising a little hell. It was a tradition to chase away evil spirits, everyone had always said.

"Supposed to be good luck to kiss under a full moon," Arjay had said. "You ever heard that?"

"No," she had said sternly but smiling at him. "Never heard tell of such thing."

"I heard that all my life," Arjay said, wise-like, the way their parents would've spoken.

"I believe you're the evil spirit I ort to be chasing away," she'd said. "If my daddy knew I's out here, Lord, God."

She wonders now if she shouldn't have gone ahead and kissed him.

"They stopped them, Mommy!" Jenny says, excitedly.

She looks up to find the van slid sideways to a stop, men tumbling out.

"Stopped who?" Sis wants to know.

"What're they doing now, baby?" Rita asks Jenny, steering carefully but gunning the engine.

"I don't know. Fighting maybe. There's a fire."

The littler one is confused and frightened, and she begins to cry. "I'm scared, Mommy."

"It's okay," Rita says in a daze. "It's just a bunch of kids playing Halloween pranks, baby. It's awright."

And then she begins to laugh. It comes ripping up out of her like a sickness that pitches her forward and makes her tremble inside. Her skin feels cold and prickly, and she's overcome all of the sudden with weakness. She feels as weak as she did just over a month ago when the baby was born. The baby, she thinks. The baby. "Check on Brother, girls."

Jenny picks the baby up and cradles him in her arms. Her eyes fill with tears and she looks at Rita in the mirror.

"Is he still hot? Feel his belly, Jen."

Jenny peels back the baby blanket and lays a hand on her brother's tummy.

"Is he hot, baby?"

The girl begins to cry. "I don't know, Mommy." Her little nerves are shot, Rita realizes. "Why don't he wake up, Mommy? What's wrong with him?"

"Why don't he wake up?" the little one parrots, and now she begins to cry again, too.

Rita's arms tremble and a sore opens up on the inside of her like the kind that must slowly eat away at the dead, she thinks, day by day supping away first the water-filled parts, the eyes, the organs, and then later the rest.

"Sing him a song," she says, her words catching in her throat. "Maybe that's what he wants."

Sis stands on the hump in the backseat, preparing to sing, and then points through the windshield. "Look," she says, "Look! Someone's coming through the underpass!" She smiles at Rita, her two front baby teeth missing, and Rita curls her arm up behind her and cups the child's face in her hand.

Jenny begins to sing softly. "The stars at night are big and bright."

"Blow your horn, Mommy!" Sis says. "Look, Mommy. See?"

"I see," Rita says, smiling wanly in the distance ahead. "Climb up here and help me," she says.

Monsters in Appalachia

She hears the dogs coming round now, bugling louder as they draw near, bawling out in unbridled rapture. Their aching bliss, laid plain, bleeds into her like a hemorrhage, and she can hear it, now, too, she thinks, calling them through the woods. Its song the furtive cry of a panther, a wailing baby. The dogs call out again, and somewhere in the quiet depths, he moans with delight as well.

Outside, it is dark as that which plagued Egypt. How the dogs manage in such blackness, she can't say, but they have a scent on their noses and that's how they go, she knows. Still, there are trees and all manner of things to watch out for in the night woods, though she guesses they can scent trees as well as beasts. Anse's Plotts are of an olden breed, the keenest ever was. They can scent things never heard tell of. Trees? Why that must be simple, she guesses. She herself can scent trees, pine rosin and fruiting pawdads, though not at a full tear through the dark.

She wishes it was light out, a whitish day with the dogs scaring up quail from the hawthorn and hedge apples. Retrieving game, not stalking it. She doesn't like the ropes of slobber that hang from their mouths after a chase such as this. Doesn't trust how they pull against their leads so hard and lust for a thing. She can hear it there now in their voices, ringing round the woods. They've treed something or hemmed something in. It is over now. They'll be home in a spell.

She goes to the stove, runs the grate back and forth, shovels out the ash, adds coal, and waits till the fire is built up good again. He'll be froze solid when he comes back. She brings clean coveralls into the canning porch, pulls on her coat, grabs the washtubs, and goes to light a fire in the yard. She is late, and here come the headlights of the truck, dogs still baying for every ounce of life they're worth, Anse's old Dodge winding out hard to drag the heavy load up the steep drive.

She drops the washtubs under the hemlock and sets a match to the kindling. Anse ties the dogs and goes back to unload his catch. She comes round after him to help.

At first, she thinks it's a bear. But it is not a bear, she knows. Too big. Unless it is a Kodiak, and she's never heard tell of Kodiak round here. Her heart mashes chamber against chamber. "Another?" she asks.

"All that's running," he replies.

"Th'ey God in heaven," she says. "Monsters. It's the end times."

"Nevertheless."

She hungers for something soft, the sweet, tender things of before. Now it is all hard hide and claw and horns and scales and beaks and necks and parts unheard of.

She looks at Anse. They string up the beast in the hemlock and split it down the middle. Bile rolls out and acid that singes what little grass there is. There is no heart inside it, nor any innards they can recognize, just what looks like a stomach, gut colored and bloated. Anse pricks it and out comes nothing but noise, low grunts, and shushed cries. She grabs it up and throws it to the dogs.

"Look what a taste for it they've got," he says. But she looks away, cannot bear it. "Did you hear it?" he asks. "Hear it wailing? You should've seen it hiss and spit at me. Look at those horns. Have you ever seen anything like it? And those wings."

"It's unclean," she says. "Take it out of here."

"Clean as any other beast," he says. "Why, look, it's an angel."

She steps closer, studies its faceless, floppy form, its veiny, segmented torso, its swine-like hoofs, cat-gut wings. "It's no angel," she says, "but a monster."

"A monster? Yes, you're right," he says. How many do you suppose there are? What all kinds, you reckon?"

* * *

He has counted and killed hundreds. Their mounted likenesses adorn the walls of the milking barn. She has never been to the barn to look, but she knows from night terrors that hell is on the other side. Worse than the monsters themselves is the smell of burning flesh, the sounds of loved ones gnashing their teeth in anguish.

"Try it," he says. "You'd get used to it if you'd just try."

"I don't want to," she says. "I'll do w'thout."

"Very well."

During the day, on her walks, she startles up quail from the hedge apples. "Look there," she says. "There they go. Oh, how I hunger. Lord, don't you know how I hunger? Oh, for the sweet, tender things still in abundance. Look there how abundant."

* * *

"I've got a shank left yet in the smokehouse," he tells her, standing to fetch it.

"No," she says, holding him from going. "Not tonight."

"I can heat it myself," he says. "Won't take but a minute."

"Don't bring that filth into my house," she says. "I've had all of it I can stand."

But he is already shaving off strips of black hindquarters with her best paring knife. "Try a bite," he says. "Look a'here," and he tosses a portion of tentacle, uncooked, into his mouth and chews.

She wonders what it tastes like, how his tongue can abide the fusty butter secreted through its pores without gagging. A yellowish smear of it collects in the corners of his mouth, and suddenly, she wants fiercely to kiss him. At their age, she thinks, cross with herself and the weakness of her flesh. She fights the urge in favor of encouraging him to talk as he eats, so she can catch the faintest scent of his breath.

* * *

At night, he sleeps like a hound. She looks at his lips and traces her cracked finger over them. She wets it and runs it over them again. It's all that's left, he told her. She looks at her finger, at his lips. She misses him. Who is this strange creature beside her? He looks the same, has the same broken capillaries crossing his nose, the same loose jowl shuddering like a spoon of preserves when he breathes. But something's different. She leans in, breathes in his breath. It's there, she thinks. Inside. She smells it. She looks into his mouth and there, his tongue. It lolls about, wide and thick as a wallet. She sees something, a line, a seam? Down the middle, yes. He smacks his lips and when she looks again, it is split. His tongue forks and flicks and she wakes herself panting.

He begins to capture and cage the monsters. He breeds them, one to the other, domesticates some that till the fields, do the hunting, work around the house. One can speak. It talks to her. Tells her *he* is the beast, that he does unspeakable things to them. "Turn me loose," it begs her. "Let me go back to my kind."

But he is a demon and she doesn't trust him. The cages are flimsy. They could all free themselves with little effort if they wanted. No, she doesn't trust them.

Outside, all around, the quail sing from the brush. "Catch me some," she begs Anse, and he sends out the speaking beast, which slaughters two hundred and brings them to her.

"Eat," the beast says. "I will bring you more, all you desire."

But she pushes it away and hides. "No."

* * *

He is lying with the beasts now. "Go and look," the speaking beast tells her.

"Get!" she says. "Leave me be." But the sounds carry on through the night. She hears his voice above the cries of the beasts. She hears him breathing, hears him humping and moaning. "God in heaven," she cries, "why do you let this go on? Speak to me. There is a demon here who speaks to me plainly, but you deny me. Again and again, Lord. Why have you forsaken me?"

* * *

He opens a sideshow called Monsters in Appalachia, where he parades the beasts by whip and chain out of the barn and onto a homemade platform built of cinder blocks and three-quarter-inch particleboard. He has identified all the ones from the book of Daniel, but he is missing a few from the book of Revelation.

"This one here," he tells curiosity seekers, "this one is a silver-tongued devil," and he cracks a whip at the one that can speak until it cries out so that the audience shrinks back in amazement.

Its voice is small now, and plaintive. She listens from the window, hears it say, "Please, master, no more."

She imagines folks leaning in to see if the thing is real or not, or maybe just for a closer look at its injuries. They don't actually believe what they're seeing. They are merely playing along for the thrill of it. Monsters in Appalachia. Foolishness.

* * *

She takes down the rifle from the rack over the doorway and sets off for the woods. The dogs have all gone mad with desire. "I will prepare a table in the wilderness," she says and sets out alone in search of quail. She is ravenous waiting on the Lord. She will go in search of Him. He has turned away from the wickedness of this place and may smite it yet, she thinks.

Outside, spectators are clapping and cheering. Carnies sell cotton candy and day-glo necklaces from tents and booths littering the fallow tobacco fields surrounding the barn. A lighted marquee stands dead center in the hayloft on which the Whore of Babylon and her Scarlet Dragon take top billing. Hand-painted banners and sackcloth signs adorn the walls of the barn, depicting the various monster acts one might see inside. "HELL ON EARTH!" says one. "POINT OF NO RETURN!"

The line of those waiting to get inside wraps around the barn. Parents and their children, a group of women wearing pastel-colored uniforms, teenagers, yuppies, coal miners, house-wives, policemen, drug dealers, car salesmen, IT geeks, Bible scholars.

The monster that can speak is talking up the acts. "Step right up. Satisfy your curiosity. Peer into oblivion. Behind this curtain, there is a legion of demons the likes of which the human mind cannot conceive. This *is* real. You will see beasts loosed on the earth thousands of years ago, bound up now for your amussee-ment." His voice is menacing, but not so much that folks are terrified. He conceals the pelt of fire-and-molten cinders covering his body and the bleeding boils beneath with a long black tunic covered in rhinestones.

At the front of the line, there stands a fierce-looking peacock-man, waving his brilliant green-blue wings, the diaphanous feathers elongated and covered in a hundred angry eyes of God. "Depart from this bed if iniquity!" issues forth from a disembodied voice. A quiver of fiery darts is strapped to the bird-man's blue-velvet shoulders and broad back, resting in the valley of the creature's wings. People step out of line to get a better look.

"Who is *that*?" they say to each other, beguiled, sore afraid for the coming of the great cataclysm rendered by the prophets.

"I am the purity of God," the peacock-man says.

The monster howls with laughter. "The purity of God, are you?"

The peacock-man speaks to the beast in harsh tones of another language, a queer bird talk. Then, more plainly, "I am Jophkiel. God will show no mercy, Sumael."

"If you are Jophkiel, the purity of God, why do you take on this preposterous disguise? Show your true form."

The line breaks and shifts into a sea of onlookers, an audience awaiting a spectacular finale. The peacock-man is awesome, they think. Is it a costume, really? They've never seen anything like it.

"'It is a wicked and evil generation that looks after a sign. There will be no sign given,' sayeth the Lord."

"Harr!" roars the speaking beast. "If you've no mysteries to reveal. Get back in line." Then he addresses the crowd. "I offer you proof. Beyond a shadow of a doubt. Step right up."

And the line rights itself again peacefully, and one by one, curiosity seekers step behind the curtain of tinkling, plinkling rhinestones suspended midair.

"Did you see them today?" he asks her in bed that night. "The excitement on their faces? The anticipation of something spectacular, impossible, unbearable?"

She does not answer, nor does he care. He is making plans. "Who was that bird-man? An actual Got-damned angel, you suppose?"

"I want a divorce," she says, and he grabs her bony wrist.

"What God has joined together, let no man put asunder."

"I never knew Him," she says.

* * *

"I have a vision," he proclaims next morning. "An outdoor drama, like *Unto These Hills*. If there are demons loose on the earth, there must be angels as well. I will find them and unleash them on the demons, and there will be Armageddon."

"Yes," she says, resting her peeling-knife hand in her lap, holding the dirt-covered spud in the other. "It's time to judge the living and the dead." This is what she's been waiting for, what they've all been yearning for fearfully but deeply. Last days, the terrible judgment.

They go together in search of the angel who had shown itself and find it whirling through the trees of the wilderness like a great gust of particlized ash.

"Messenger of the Lord," Anse says, falling on his face on the leaf-moldering floor of the forest. "Go and unlock the gates of heaven so that the Creator can separate the righteous from the unrighteous."

At once, a blinding light shines forth more radiant than the sun, and a voice says, "What have you to sacrifice?"

"Nothing," Anse says, black tears burning hot in his eye sockets, leaving blisters on his bearded old jowls. "All that I have and am is misery. My wife there is an adulteress, and I am a sorcerer."

"Even so, the Creator requires a burnt offering. Bring it here and I will intercede on your behalf."

* * *

At home again, they sit on the davenport and gaze into the conjure box, which makes light of wars and disease and pestilence plaguing the earth. The weight of their transgressions is made both heavier and lighter now by their confession. She walks to the stove and stares at the fiery coals. It is good to deny one's self, she thinks.

* * *

In the beginning, the earth was formless and void, and darkness was on the face of the deep. And God gave dominion to man, who bore woman of his own flesh. And the woman was tempted by the formless void and the darkness that roamed. So she ate, and he ate what she ate, and they were cast out of the garden forever.

* * *

"I have learnt my lesson," she says. "I shall never eat another bite of anything but that what has been bought by the blood of the Lamb."

"Then you sh'll starve, woman," Anse says. "I aim to be fed one way or a'tother." He and the speaking beast sit at the table spread with the meat of their own kind.

"I will never pull up a ch'eer to a table such as that again.

Hold my hand to Jesus," she says, clutching a dishtowel to her breast with one hand, lifting the other up to heaven.

"Then you shall perish," says the beast, smiling coolly, "and suffer the terrible judgment."

"I welcome it," says she, unhinging a deranged smile, wringing the dishcloth in her hands. "I give up my whole self, my wretched old body and twisted, black heart. I want nary a piece of it no more."

Suddenly, a form moves beneath the earth and buckles the kitchen floor, tearing asunder the shoe-scuffed linoleum that curls at the walls' edges.

"I would gladly take my place in purgatory but for the terrible great judgment of the Lord to come!" She hollers excitedly at the sight of her house being rent to pieces, the windows now twisting and warping and shattering out of their frames.

"I'd cast my own soul into the fiery furnace of hell but for the righteousness of God to be revealed! I'd cast the whole lot of mankind there with me—we none of us deserves no better—but for the glory of Jesus Christ, the gentle Lamb, the ter-rible judge, to rain down His purifying fire from heaven and burn us ever' one to cinders!"

"I would consume the tick-ridden hide of the devil his self to make right what wrong I done," she says, flailing her arms round about her and letting her head flop back.

The little shack crumbles to the mountainside around them, and now Anse, too, begins to plead to the Heavenly Host to render forth the great ending. "Come, Yahweh, come!"

The blue halo that surrounds the earth becomes gauzy. The sky fills with ice shavings and dust, an astral mirror moving over the face of the waters and the firmament, and over all the herbs that yield seeds and trees that bear fruit, over all the fish that swim in the waters and all the winged birds that fill the air, over all the cattle and creeping things. And the reflection of the whole world is turned upside down and cast up into the sky.

And every eye on the earth and in the ground and in the sea gazes up and looks at its likeness in the sky, and it sees its whole self, from continent to continent, every mountain, every stream, every tree and rock and animal, and between those, every shadow, every dark moving place the eye has ever been tempted by. And beyond that the vastness of space. The blue halo thins further and the sky turns sallow with saltpeter. And a whisper goes out over all the earth, calling every creature by its name.

Reading and Discussion Questions

1. Many of the stories in the collection deal with themes of good and evil. Which biblical allusions and symbols stand out to you most? What, if anything, do you think the author is suggesting?

2. Does the title story, "Monsters in Appalachia," represent the rest of the book? What does the author seem to be suggesting about monsters? In what ways are characters in the book monsters? In what ways are we?

3. The stories range in style from realist, historical depictions of Appalachia to magical realism and the surreal. Many of the images are stark or sometimes grotesque or farcical. Is the author pointing out certain absurdities in this cultural landscape? Are these absurdities exclusive to Appalachia, or do they exist elsewhere as well?

4. Many of the characters are affected by poverty. In what ways has poverty determined their fates? Would their lives have played out differently under different circumstances? Which characters have been most impacted?

5. The author often shines the spotlight on female characters. How are women depicted in the book? In what ways are they limited by their circumstances? Which characters rise above these limitations? Which ones capitulate?

6. Characters are often depicted as reckless or dangerous. To what degree does place create a sense of desperation in characters? Are there similarities to how men and women are portrayed? Differences? Is the author playing with stereotypes, or are we given accurate illustrations of the different ways that men and women sometimes deal with the circumstances of their lives? How does gender, time, and place determine characters' actions?

7. Desire and temptation feature prominently throughout the collection. Which characters come to mind? Describe the extent to which desire is synonymous with sin? Why is that?

8. Appalachia is often ridiculed and stereotyped. How does the author address certain stereotypes?

9. To what degree is Appalachia depicted as a haunted landscape? Why do you think the author paints a portrait of Appalachia that feels worlds apart from anywhere else? Is this an accurate portrayal? Are characters trapped by the landscape, or is the landscape trapped by the characters?

10. Many of the stories in the collection are dark, but they're often punctuated by moments of light. Consider the final two paragraphs of the book. Despite the characters' sorrows, is there a sense of redemption or hope?

About the Author

Sheryl Monks holds an MFA from Queens University of Charlotte. Her work has earned the Reynolds Price Short Fiction Award and has appeared in the *Greensboro Review*, *Midwestern Gothic*, *storySouth*, *Regarding Arts & Letters*, and elsewhere. She is a founding editor of *Change Seven* magazine. Learn more at sherylmonks.com.

CPSIA information can be obtained
at www.ICGtesting.com
Printed in the USA
LVOW04s1223071016
507738LV00004B/4/P